WAR

Also by Louis-Ferdinand Céline
AVAILABLE FROM NEW DIRECTIONS

Death on the Installment Plan

Guignol's Band

Journey to the End of the Night

LOUIS-FERDINAND CÉLINE

War

*translated from the French
by Charlotte Mandell*

A NEW DIRECTIONS
PAPERBOOK ORIGINAL

Originally published as *Guerre* in 2022.
Published by arrangement with Éditions Gallimard.

ACKNOWLEDGMENT
The translator would like to thank Éric Trudel,
Odile Chilton, and Allan Kausch for their help.

Published as New Directions Paperbook 1601 in 2024
Manufactured in the United States of America.

Library of Congress Cataloging-in-Publication Data
Names: Céline, Louis-Ferdinand, 1894–1961, author. |
Mandell, Charlotte, translator.
Title: War / Louis-Ferdinand Céline ; translated by Charlotte Mandell.
Other titles: Guerre. English
Description: First edition. | New York : New Directions Publishing Corp., 2024.
Identifiers: LCCN 2024004635 | ISBN 9780811237321 (paperback)
| ISBN 9780811237338 (ebook)
Subjects: LCSH: World War, 1914–1918—Fiction. | LCGFT: War fiction. | Novels.
Classification: LCC PQ2607.E834 G7913 2024 |
DDC 843/.91—dc23/eng/20240312
LC record available at https://lccn.loc.gov/2024004635

2 4 6 8 10 9 7 5 3 1

New Directions Books are published for James Laughlin
by New Directions Publishing Corporation
80 Eighth Avenue, New York 10011

Contents

PUBLISHER'S NOTE vii

WAR 1

INDEX OF RECURRENT CHARACTERS 107

Publisher's note

When he fled for his life in 1944 from Paris, an abhorred collaborator and the author of a number of viciously anti-Semitic works, Céline left behind more than five thousand pages of manuscripts. They vanished, and he long claimed they'd been stolen, but only in 2020 did a journalist make public their existence. Whoever originally had taken them preserved them and apparently did not want Céline's widow Lucette (who died in 2019 at the age of 107) to profit by their publication. Gallimard's *inédit* edition of *Guerre,* overseen by Pascal Fouché, was published in 2022.

The manuscript of *Guerre* was transcribed from a handwritten and "well preserved" first draft: it did not receive the rigorous revising process that the author usually undertook. Readers of *War* will note instances of missing text such as "[illegible word]." Inconsistencies—such as the sudden appearance of "Agathe" at the end and the metamorphosis of the name of Ferdinand's friend Bébert to Cascade, and then back again—have likewise been retained. (Curiously, Bébert was the name of the cat Céline carried when he escaped with his wife and with some gold sewn into her clothing.) The racist term for North Africans, *bicots*, has been left in the original French here. An index of recurrent characters can be found on page 107.

WAR

I must have been lying there for part of the following night as well. My whole left ear was stuck to the ground with blood, my mouth too. Between the two there was an immense noise. I slept in the noise and then it rained, hard. Kersuzon next to me was stretched out heavy under the water. I moved one arm toward his body. Touched it. The other one I couldn't. I didn't know where my other arm was. It had flown into the air, twisted in space, then fallen back down and jabbed into my shoulder, in the raw part of the meat. It made me scream at the top of my lungs every time and then it got worse. Afterwards, though still shouting, I managed to make less noise than the horrific din bashing my head in, on the inside, like a train. It didn't do any good to resist. This was the first time in that whole nightmare full of shells whistling by that I slept, in all the noise that was possible, without entirely losing consciousness—that is, in horror. Except for a few hours when they operated on me, I never completely lost consciousness. Since December '14, I've always slept like that—in excruciating noise. I caught the war in my head. It's locked up inside my head.

So. I was saying that in the middle of the night, I turned over onto my stomach. That worked. I learned to tell the difference between the outside noises and the noises that would never leave me. As for pain, I had my fill of it in my shoulder and knee. Still, I managed to stand up. Despite everything I was hungry. I turned around a little in the sort of enclosure where with Le Drellière and the convoy we'd met our end. Where could he be at that moment? And the others? Hours, a whole night, and almost an entire day had passed since we'd come to crush them. They were nothing more now than little heaps on the slope and in the orchard where our carts were smoking, crackling and fire-blazing. The big forge wagon was still getting thoroughly charred, the cart even more so. I didn't recognize the sergeant in the middle. Further on I recognized one of the horses with something behind it, a piece of shaft, in the embers, flung against the wall of the farmhouse that had just collapsed into rubble. They must have come galloping back into the wreckage in the middle of it all, driven ass-first by the shelling, no other way to put it, straight into the machine-gun fire. He'd worked hard, La Drellière. I stayed crouched in the same spot. The shells had done a thorough job of pulverizing the mud. At least two hundred shells had rained down. Dead bodies scattered all over the place. The guy carrying the haversacks had exploded like a grenade, no other way to put it, from his neck to the middle of his pants. In his belly there were already two leisurely rats snacking on his haversack, squatting on their haunches. Everything in the enclosure stank of rotting meat and burning, but especially the pile in the middle where there were at least ten horses, all of them ripped open, their bodies mingled. That's where he'd finished his gallop, pierced by a heavy mortar shell, or three, that hit a few feet away. The memory of the bag of cash La Drellière had on him suddenly came to mind, from deep within my smashed-up head.

I didn't really know what to think. I wasn't in a state to think too hard. Still, despite all the horror I found myself in, the cash worried the hell out of me, on top of the deafening noise I was carrying around in this shitty adventure, the noise seemed to be hanging around more there than me. I wasn't sure I could hear the cannon in the distance either. It was all mixed up together. In the distance I saw little groups on horseback or on foot, moving away. I'd have liked them to be Germans, but they didn't come any closer. No doubt they had other things to fuck up in other directions. They must have been following orders. Here the terrain must have been used up for fighting. It was just up to me—I had to find the regiment. Where could it be? In order to think, even a tiny bit, I had to start over and over again, like when you're talking to someone on a platform as a train's passing. One scrap of thought at a time, intensely, one after the other. It's a tiring exercise, I can assure you. By now I'm an expert. After twenty years, you learn. My mind is harder, like my biceps. I believe more in abilities. I've learned how to make music, how to sleep, how to forgive, and, see, how to write fine literature as well, all with little pieces of horror ripped from the noise that will never end. Anyway.

In the rubble of the big forge wagon there were some cans of corned beef. Blown up by the fire, but still good enough for me. But then there's thirst. Everything I wolfed down with one hand was full of blood, mine of course and others'. So I looked for a corpse that still had some booze on him. I found it at the far end, next to the enclosure's exit, on a chasseur on a dead horse. In his coat there was some Bordeaux, two bottles even. Stolen of course, an officer's Bordeaux. Afterwards I headed east, where we came from. A hundred yards at a time. I began to feel I was starting to see more clearly where things were. I thought I could spot a horse in the middle of the field. I wanted to ride it but when I got close, it was just a swollen cow, three days dead. That of course made me more tired. Soon I also saw some artillery that surely didn't exist. Nothing was the same anymore, with my ear the way it was.

I still hadn't come across any actual poilus. Some more miles. I swallowed some more blood. As for noise it was calming down a little in my head. But then I vomited it all up, including both bottles. Everything was spinning. I said to myself, shit, Ferdinand. You're going to die, just when you've gotten through the worst of it!

Never have I been so brave. And then I thought of the bag of cash, of all the regiment's vans thoroughly looted, and then I hurt in three different places all at once, in my arm, in my whole head with the horrible noise, and, even more profoundly, in my mind. I was in a panic because deep down I'm really a nice boy. I would have talked to myself out loud if my tongue hadn't still been plastered down with blood. That usually gives me courage.

The land there was flat—but the deep, treacherous ditches, full of water, made it hard to go forward. You had to keep making endless detours, only to end up in the same spot. And I thought I could hear some bullets whining. But the water trough I'd stopped next to must have been a real one. I was holding one arm with the other because I couldn't keep it straight anymore. It was dead at my side. At shoulder level there was a sort of big sponge made of cloth and blood. If I moved it a little I'd stop living, it caused such a searing pain all the way down—no other way to put it—into life itself.

I felt the life that was still inside me, that was defending itself so to speak. I'd never have thought that possible if someone had told me. I was even walking pretty well now, or at least a thousand feet at a time. The pain was excruciating everywhere, from below my knee to inside my head. Aside from that my ears were full of an echoing mishmash of sounds, and things were not entirely the same as they'd been before, either. Everything seemed to be made of putty, the trees didn't look steady at all, the road under my boots rose and fell. I had nothing on me except my tunic and the rain. Still no one. In the wide-open empty countryside, I could hear the torture in my head that much louder. It almost made me afraid to hear myself. I thought I was going to wake up the battle, I was making so much noise inside. I was making more noise in my head than a battle. In a flash of sunlight in the distance, a real bell tower looms up over the fields, a huge one. Go that way, I tell myself. One destination is as good as another. And then I sit down—with the enormous din in my head, my arm in shreds, and I try to remember what had just happened. I couldn't. When it came to memory, there was nothing but a jumble. And to begin with I was too hot, the bell tower kept changing its distance, it appeared close up, then farther away. Maybe it's a mirage, I say to myself. But I'm not such an idiot. Since I'm in such pain all over, the bell tower must exist too. That's one way to reason, to get your faith back. So I set off again, walking on the side of the road. At a bend, a guy way out in the mud beyond stirs, he must see me. I think it's a corpse wriggling, I must be seeing things. He was dressed in yellow with a rifle, I'd never seen anyone rigged out like him before. The guy was shaking or maybe I was. He motions for me to come over. So I do. I wasn't risking anything. Then he talks to me from up close. I realize right away. He's English. In the state I was, it seemed fantastic that he was English. With my mouth full of blood I answer him right away in English, it even comes naturally. Me, who hadn't wanted to cough up ten words when I was over there to learn it, I start making conversation with the guy in yellow. Emotion no doubt. It did me good, even my ears, to speak English with him. I felt there was less noise between them. So he helps me walk. He supports me very carefully. I paused often. I think it's better, when it comes down to it, that he's the one who found me instead of some bastard from back home. At least with him I didn't have to go over the whole story about what had happened to our expedition.

"Where are we going?" I asked in English ...

"To Yprèss!" he said.

Yprèss, that must be over there with the bell tower. So it was real, a city church tower. There was still another four hours' march, hopping as I was, on paths and especially across fields. I could see more clearly but I saw red if I looked up. My whole body was divided into parts. The wet part, the drunk part, the arm part that was excruciating, the ear part that was abominable, the friendship part with the English guy which was very comforting, then the part of the knee that kept randomly dislocating itself, the part of the past that was already trying, I remember, to cling to the present but couldn't—and then the future, which made me more afraid than everything else, a comic part that wanted to drown out the others and tell me a story. You can't even call that suffering anymore, it was just comical. After we walked another mile, I refused to go any farther.

"Where were you going?" I asked him all of a sudden, just as a point of curiosity.

I stop. I refuse to go any further. It's not that far away, though, his Ypres. The fields were rolling all around us, swelling in fat moving humps as if giant rats were lifting clumps of earth as they moved below the furrows. Maybe even people. It was huge, an army seemingly just under the earth ... It was moving like the sea in actual waves ... Better for me to sit still. Especially since when I move it's with all the noise of the storm raging between my temples. There was nothing in my head except the blast of a hurricane. Suddenly I screamed.

"I am not going! I am going to the War of Movement!" I shouted.

And I did as I said. I got up again with my arm and my ear, blood everywhere, and I set off in the direction of the enemy line we'd started out from. So then my comrade bawled me out and I understood all the words. My fever must have been rising, and the hotter I got the more easily I could understand English.

I was staggering but I was stubborn, putting on a brave front. He couldn't figure out how to stop me. So there we were in the middle of the field, having a scene so to speak. Fortunately there was no one there to watch us. Finally he was the one who won, he grabbed me by the arm, the one that was gaping open. So he was bound to win. I followed him. But we hadn't gone a quarter of an hour toward the town I see on ahead, when there came toward us a good dozen cavalrymen in khaki. From seeing them so close up I start imagining things, that the battle's going to start up again.

"Hooray!" I yell as soon as I see them: "Hooray!"

"Hooray!" they reply.

Now I knew they were English.

Their officer comes over to us. He compliments me.

"Brave soldier! Brave soldier!" he says. "Where do you come from?"

I'd stopped thinking about that, where I came from. He was making me afraid again, the bastard.

I wanted to clear off again, from what was ahead and what was behind, both ways. The comrade who had taken charge of me gave me a big kick in the ass, toward the city. No one wanted me to be brave anymore. As for me I didn't know where to set my sights, ahead or behind, and inside I hurt too much. Le Drellière hadn't seen any of that. He had died too soon. In a little while the road positively rose up toward me, gently, a real kiss I could say, up to eye level and I lay down on it like in a very soft bed with the massive shells exploding in my skull and everything. And then it calmed down some and the soldiers' horses came toward me, I mean their stupid gallop, since I didn't see anyone.

When I recovered my sort-of-mind, I was in a church, on an actual bed. I woke up to the noise in my ears again, and to the sound of a dog I thought was eating my left arm. I didn't dwell on it. Unless they opened up my belly all raw and without anesthesia, I couldn't hurt more all over. It lasted not an hour but all night long. I saw a strange movement in the shadow below my eyes, all soft and all melodious, which somehow awakened something in me.

I couldn't believe it. It was a dame's arm. Despite everything it gave my zozo a real hard-on. I looked with one eye for the place where her butt was. Between the bedsteads I saw her rear end undulating back and forth on the taut cloth. Like a dream starting all over again. Life has its tricks. Ideas arose all askew, tangled up, and they followed her ass, expectantly. They rolled me over to a corner of the church, a corner full of light. There I passed out again probably because of the smell, it must have been to put me to sleep. Two days must have passed, with more pain, huge noises in my big head, nothing but real life. It's funny I remember that time. It's not so much that I went through hell that I remember—it was more that, like an idiot, I wasn't responsible for anything at all, not even for my prick. It was more than appalling, it was shameful. It was the whole person that you've been given, which you've defended in the uncertain, atrocious, already hardened past, all that was so ridiculous in those moments, in the process of falling apart and then running after the pieces. I was looking at it—life—as it was almost torturing me. When it puts me through the agony of death for good, I'll spit in its face just like that. It's completely idiotic starting from a certain point, you can't fool me, I know life too well. I've seen it. We'll find each other again. We have unfinished business. Life can fuck off.

But I have to tell everything. After three days, a shell hit the main altar, a real one. The English who were in charge of the field hospital decided we should all get out. I wasn't too keen on that. This church had shapes that also moved, hollyhock pillars that twined around in the yellow and green of the stained-glass windows, as at a festival. We drank lemonade from baby bottles. It was all good in one way. I mean in the area where liquids pass. I had a nightmare—I even saw trotting by high up in the vaults, on a horse with wings made all of gold, General Métuleu des Entrayes who was surely looking for me ... He stared at me, tried to recognize me, and then his mouth moved and his mustache began fluttering like a butterfly.

"I've changed, haven't I, Métuleu?" I asked him quietly, familiarly.

And then I fell asleep despite everything, with one more anxiety, very clear, nestled just between the eye sockets and which reached even deeper to the bottom of ideas, even further than the noise, enormous as it was, which I keep describing over and over.

They must have transported us to the train station and then we set off in the train. They were cattle cars. They still reeked of fresh manure. It rolled along quite gently. Not so long ago we'd arrived from the other direction to wage war. One, two, three, four months already had passed. In my car were nothing but stretchers the whole length, in two rows. I was near the door. There was another stench, I knew that well too, the stench of the dead, and of antiseptic. They must have evacuated us urgently from the field hospital.

"Hey ... hey!" I called out like a cow as soon as I woke up a little—it was the place for that.

No one replied at first. We were advancing inch by inch so to speak. But after my third try, two guys in the back answered:

"Hey, hey! That's a good shout for our wounded asses. It's so easy to say."

Choo, choo ... from far away, it must have been the engine going uphill. The explosions in my ear tricked me more. Everything came to a halt by a river that was streaming from the moon, then we started up again rattling. It was almost exactly like the way out really. It reminded me of Péronne. I wondered which recruits could still be lying there in the cattle cars, if they were French or English, or Belgian maybe.

Since the whole world understands Hey, hey!, I started up again.

No more replies. Except, the ones who'd been groaning, they'd stopped groaning. All except one who kept repeating "Marie," with a sort of accent and also a gurgling sound right next to me— definitely a guy who was emptying himself out of his mouth. I knew that tone too. In two months I'd learned pretty much all the sounds of the earth and of men. We stayed there a good two hours, motionless on the embankment in the freezing cold. Just the *choo choo* of the locomotive. And then a cow too saying— much louder than me before—*moo moo* in a meadow out ahead of us. I answered her to see. She must have been hungry. We moved forward a little *vroom, vroom* ... All the wheels, all kinds of flesh, all the ideas on Earth were piling up together in the noise in the back of my head. At that moment though I told myself it was all over. That that was enough. I pushed one foot onto the floor. It stayed firm. I turned over. I even sat up. I looked at the shadows of the train car, in front, behind. I blinked. There were bodies that had stopped moving under the stretcher blankets. There were two rows of stretchers. I tried:

"Hey hey."

No one answered then. Standing up, I held firm too, not for long but long enough to reach the doors. With one arm I opened them more ... I sat down on the edge in the dark. It was exactly like when we'd gone up to the war but now we were going even more slowly back down. There weren't any horses on the train now. It must have been very cold, it was definitely not summer anymore but I was just as hot and thirsty as I'd be in summer, and also I was seeing things in the dark. And because of my noises I even heard voices and also there were entire columns passing by on the fields, marching six feet above the ground. It was definitely their turn. They were all going up to war. Me, I was coming back from it. Ours was a pretty small cattle car, but when I think about it, there were a good fifteen dead men inside. Maybe we could still hear a cannon very far away. It must have been the same for the other cars. *Choo! Choo!* It was a little locomotive that must have been having a hard time dragging all this. We were going behind the lines. If I stay with them, I said to myself, I'm dead for real, but I hurt so bad, and there's so much noise in my head, that in one sense dying would have done me good. Finally—the corpse that was on the stretcher in the back on the right—I saw his face all of a sudden, and then the faces of the others too, since our carriage had just stopped under a gas lamp. That got me talking, seeing them.

"Hey, hey!" I said to everyone.

And then the train crawled some more to the very edge of the open country, to a meadow all covered in mud so thick that I said to myself: Ferdinand you're going to walk on that like at home.

And I walked on it. I set straight off into this eiderdown, no other way to put it. I was wrapped in cloud everywhere. That's it, I said, this time I'm deserting for good. I sat down, it was wet. A little further on I saw the walls of the city already, high walls—a real fortress protecting it. A big city in the North no doubt. I'll sit down in front of it, I say. Now I was saved, I wasn't alone anymore. I take on a cunning look. Kersuzon, Keramplech, Gargader and the boy Le Cam were around me, in a circle as it were. Only, their eyes were closed. They were reproaching me. In short they'd come to keep watch over me. We'd been together for almost four years! But I'd never deceived them. Gargader was pouring blood from the middle of his forehead. It was turning all the fog beneath him red. I even pointed it out to him. Kersuzon, it's true, was completely armless, but big ears to listen with. The boy Le Cam—you could see daylight through his head, through his eyes as if through field glasses. That's funny. Keramplech had grown himself a beard, his hair was as long as a lady's, he'd kept his helmet and he was paring his nails with the tip of a bayonet. He was doing that to listen to me too. He had guts that were sliding from his ass far into the countryside. I had to talk to them, otherwise they'd surely report me. The war, I said, it's going on in the north. It's not here at all. They said nothing.

King Krogold went back home: just as I said that there was cannon fire through the countryside.* I pretended not to hear. It isn't real, I said. We sang together, all four of us: King Krogold went back home! We sang out of tune. I spat on Kersuzon's face, all red. The idea came then, a good one. It was beautiful. We were in front of Christiania. That's my opinion even now. On the road, from the south that is, it's Thibaut and Joad coming toward me. In funny outfits too, rags to tell the truth. They too were coming to Christiania, to loot maybe. You'll get a fever, you swine! That's what I shouted. Kersuzon and the others didn't dare contradict me. I was the corporal after all, even after what had happened. I'm still the one who knows, to desert or not. You had to know everything.

"Tell us," I said to Gargader Yvon who was from that region. "It's Thibaut who killed him, old Morvan, Joad's father," I said, "he's the one who killed him. Tell us," I said. "Tell me further, sooner I mean. Tell me how he killed him, with a dagger, a rope, a saber? No? With a big rock to smash in his face?"

* "King Krogold" is an allusion to *La volonté du roi Krogold,* which Céline wrote and used in *Mort à credit* (*Death on the Installment Plan*). See the index of recurrent characters, p. 105.

"That's right," Gargader replied. "Completely accurate, word for word."

Old Morvan had given Thibaut a little money so he'd keep quiet, so he wouldn't take his son far away, off to the adventure, so he'd leave the boy alone to spend all his life by Morvan's side in Terdigonde in the Vendée, like us before, in Romanches in the Somme, where we were so bored on the 22nd before the war. One day Joad's old man must have invited people over, powerful, rich guests, people from the Parliament, getting shitfaced at his house. He was drunk too, old Morvan, a little more than the others even, drunk enough to puke. He'd left his place at the banquet to lean out the window. In the alley below there wasn't anyone yet. Yes, a little cat, a big rock. Thibaut was just arriving, rounding the corner.

"He won't come, your friend. He won't come to amuse us, to play his instrument for us, he's been paid though. He took twenty *écus* from me in advance ... He's a thief that Thibaut, I've always said so."

At that instant Thibaut who'd heard him stood up with the big rock in his hand and struck old Morvan dead with a single blow right on his temple. So the insult was utterly avenged in the end. Terrible. Just like that, his soul left. Like the sound of a heavy bell on the first blow, it flew away.

Thibaut entered the house with the pilgrims. They buried the prosecutor three days later. Ma Morvan, very sad, didn't suspect a thing. In the dead man's very bedroom Thibaut sat, like a friend. And then with Joad he'd gone off to do the rounds of all the taverns. And then they'd had enough, both of them. Joad could think of nothing but distant love affairs, of Wanda the princess, the daughter of King Krogold, even farther north from Christiania, on top of Morehande. Thibaut wanted nothing but adventures, even the wealthy house couldn't keep him there. He had killed for nothing, just for the pleasure of it in short. Now they've both set off. We see them crossing Brittany like Gargader before them, leaving Terdigonde in the Vendée forever like Keramplech.

"Isn't that good," I said to my three revolting companions, "isn't my story beautiful?"

They said nothing at first, and finally it was Cambelech, who'd gone behind me, who spoke. I wasn't expecting him: his face was all split in two, his lower jaw was hanging in disgusting shreds.

Using both hands to make his mouth work, "Corporal," he said like that: "We're not happy, no we're not, that's not the kind of story we need ..."*

* At the end of this section, Gallimard notes: "The manuscript contains another page which is obviously not in the right place, since Ferdinand is told he'll be operated on the next day, which happens only in the second section. Since it can't be inserted anywhere in this manuscript, it probably belongs to another version of the text. Here's the transcription: 'Watch out!' I shouted then. 'Watch out!' I screamed even more loudly./ 'Calm down my friend,' the lady replies, 'calm down ... Everything's OK ... drink this and then you won't be operated on till tomorrow morning.'/ These things were happening in the Parfaite-Miséricorde Hospital on January 22, 1915 in Noirceur-sur-la-Lys around four in the afternoon."

No one could have been more out of it. But it was still far from easy, since it wasn't till two days later that they collected me, lying in the field below where I'd slid, after I let myself slip from the train car. I was off my rocker for sure. They took me to the hospital. They had to think about it first before deciding. They didn't know if I was Belgian or English, and they weren't sure I was French either, my uniform was so shredded, just from getting that far. I could have been German, there was no way for them to tell. There were enough kinds for all tastes in the Peurdu-sur-la-Lys hospitals.* It was a little town but well situated to receive conscripts from all the battles. They put some labels on my belly and then finally I ended up on the rue des Trois-Capucines at the Virginal Secours, which was run by society ladies as well as nuns. It wasn't the best place to wind up at, as I'll show later. In one way it pissed me off that I was doing better because I had to make an effort to appear out of it as they were transporting me. It wasn't so sincere. In short the two days and nights in the grass had mostly done me good, given me some fucking vitality. I looked around a little from my stretcher and saw that the guys who were taking me into town were male nurses with white hair. As for the pain and noise, the whistling and the whole racket, it had all come back the moment I was conscious again, but it was bearable. Though I still preferred the complete dilapidation from before, when I was almost dead, except for this shitload of pain, music, and ideas. Now there was no doubt that if they talked to me there was

* Peurdu-sur-Lys: a pun on "peur," *fear*, and "perdu," *lost*.

nothing to stop me from answering. That's always the difficult thing, despite the fact that my mouth was still full of blood and even the cotton wool plugging up my left ear. The trick with the dream about the fairytale I could no longer be sly enough to use, I couldn't deliver it cold, since now with my chill I was shaking. I was as cold as a dead man in short, but just cold. It wasn't going well. They took me through the town gates and over a real drawbridge, very cautiously. We passed some officers and even a general and then some Englishmen, lots of soldiers, cafés, barber shops. Horses that they were taking to the water trough, that reminded me of a thousand things. I looked over all these things, remembering Romanches. How many months since we'd left? It was as if we'd gone through a whole world, as if we'd fallen from the moon ...

I soaked in everything about this new place. There was no way I could be any uglier or more repulsive than I was, but still I was immediately on my guard, those bastard excuses for men would still want a piece of me, even if I was nothing but a bloody slab of meat, a thundering ear, a big fat capitulating head, I'd still be hunted down, even more cruelly than ever.

"OK Ferdinand," I said, "you didn't croak in time, you're a fine coward, you fucking loser, so much for your stupid filthy ass."

I wasn't wrong about much. I'm gifted with imagination, I can say so without offense. I'm not afraid of reality anymore either, but with everything that was happening at Peurdu-sur-la-Lys there was enough to make several battalions feverish. No questions. I'll explain. You'll judge for yourselves. In these cases as well, you follow your own advice. You head toward whatever hope you still have left. It doesn't shine very brightly, hope, a thin candle ring at the very end of an utterly hostile infinite corridor. You make do.

"This way, please."

We've arrived. The nurses put me in the basement.

"He's in a coma!" the very appealing broad announces. "Leave him alone, we'll wait and see …"

I make some noises through my nose when I hear these remarks. I'm suddenly petrified they'll chuck me all raw into one of the crates. I see crates and trestles. Suddenly the skirt comes back.

"I told you, he's in a coma!"

Then she asks:

"There's nothing in his bladder at least?"

That seems a bizarre question to me, woozy as I am. The porter guys didn't know anything about my bladder. In fact I did want to piss. I let it go, it streams from the stretcher and then onto the tiled floor. This the dame sees. In one gesture she opens up my pants. Fondles my romeo. The guys leave to look for another pathetic case. Then the broad explores my pants with more precision. Believe it or not, I get hard. I didn't want to seem so dead that they'd box me up, but I didn't want to have a hard-on either so that they'd think I was an impostor. But nothing doing: the lady was groping me so thoroughly that I squirm. I half open one eye. It was a room with white curtains, a tiled floor. Then I see them clearly on the left and right, the stretchers covered in stiff sheets. I'm not mistaken. They were there. Also on trestles, other coffins arriving. It wasn't the time to be mistaken.

"Make an effort Ferdinand, you're in exceptional circumstances. You're a deceiver, deceive."

The broad must have found me attractive, right away. She wasn't repelled. She didn't let go of my zobar. I say to myself: should I smile, or not? Should I seem friendly or out of it? To cover all the bases, I stammer. It's less risky. I take up my ditty:

"I want to go to Morehande …!" I intone in a singsong through the congealed blood … "I'll go to see King Krogold … I'll go on the great crusade all alone …"

Suddenly the skirt picks up the pace, she gives me a real hard-on, reassured no doubt that I'm kidding, only I hurt my arm which I wiggle like a kid. I shout a little, and then I shoot my load, she has her hands full, notices I'm not opening my eyes anymore, she wipes me with some cotton. I'm delirious, that's all. Other women come in. I ogle. Virginal types. I hear my skirt saying:

"You should catheterize this one, come here Mademoiselle Cotydon, you'll learn something, he has something in his bladder too, this one ... Dr. Méconille recommended it highly before he left ... 'Catheterize the wounded who have trouble urinating ... Catheterize the wounded ...'"

They take me up to the first floor then, ostensibly to catheterize me. I'm a little reassured. I look around. No coffins on the first floor. Nothing but beds, between folding screens.

Four of the ladies gather around to undress me. First they get me wet from head to foot, soaking all my rags because everything's stuck together, from hair to socks. My feet have become part of the leather. Those maneuvers are painful. In my arm I have maggots, I can see them squirming, I can feel them. Suddenly the Cotydon chick feels a little sick. The broad who jerked me off takes over. She's not too bad, the jerker-off, except for her teeth which protrude and are slightly green too, with a little rotten spot. But that doesn't matter. The whole scene seems caring and as it should be. I open my eyes, but keep them fixed on the ceiling.

"Death to Gwendor the treacherous, death to the treacherous Germans ... Death to the invaders of poor Belgium!"

I holler crazily at the top of my lungs. I'm being careful, they're staring at me ... There are still four of them.

"He's still delirious, the poor wretch. Bring me the necessary things. I'll catheterize him myself," the jerker-off says.

"Yes Mademoiselle, I'll bring the catheter things right away."

They left me alone with this person. What was said was done.

Seriously though—she scraped the inside of my prick. It wasn't a joke anymore. I didn't get hard. I didn't dare to scream. Then she bandaged me, put new dressings on my head, ear, and arm, fed me liquids from a spoon and then left me alone.

"Get some rest," the catheterizer-in-chief said, "and soon Captain Boisy Jousse, the administrative officer, will come and ask you some questions. If of course you're in a state to answer him, and then tonight Dr. Méconille will come by..."

There was a future. I didn't care to be "in a state," as she said, to answer. Boisy Jousse I said nothing to at first. It's very simple, for almost ten days they thought whatever they wanted. I had no papers on me. I had nothing but my crooked bleeding face, my insides much worse, same story for all the rest, and that's it. I was much more afraid of being re-catheterized. It was a mania. Mademoiselle L'Espinasse is the catheterizer's name, she's the one who's in charge of everything. They found me feverish that night, that did me good. I wasn't getting gangrene, I only just felt like I was. Still the question was whether they were going to isolate me downstairs with the dying or not. L'Espinasse was probably getting tired of catheterizing me and jerking me off. Except one night the doctor didn't come by, he was busy, and she slipped between the beds and kissed my forehead on the sly behind the screen. So I reciprocated with a little piece of murmured poetry... like when you expire...

"Wanda, stop waiting for your betrothed, Gwendor isn't waiting for a savior anymore... Joad, your courage-less heart... Thibaut I see approaching from the North... Far to the north of Morehande, Krogold is coming... to take me away..."

Then I made a gurgling sound, and I even knew enough to spit some blood by blowing hard through my nose. She dabbed beneath my nostrils with a compress and then kissed me again. She was a passionate one deep down. I didn't understand her character very well but I figured I'd need her, the old girl, later on. And I was right.

Dr. Méconille the next day, as soon as he saw me, he gets excited observing me. He wanted to operate on me on the double, that very night he said. L'Espinasse was against it because of my exhaustion. I think that's what saved me. If I understood him right, he wanted to remove the bullet right away from behind the back of my ear. She didn't want him to. As for me, just from looking at Méconille I was sure that as soon as he started in on my head, it was all over. As soon as he left, the gals around L'Espinasse told her she was right to have resisted, "that he's a doctor, not a surgeon, Méconille, and it's just to get some practice that he wants to operate on him, he should start with the easy cases first. The war'll last long enough ... there's time, and anyway, he could try to patch up the bone in his arm first, it's also broken, but the head's too complicated for him ... he shouldn't start there ... " As for me, the fact is that when they'd shown me the little lazaretto down in the basement when I arrived, it had given me an additional terror, they'd filled me with panic first thing. If they hadn't shown me the little lazaretto with the trestles and the two coffins on top I might not have been so stubborn, I might have given in, but because I knew everything, because I'd seen the caskets, I made a supreme effort to resist. It was the rotting stench of the dead bodies that disgusted me about the lazaretto. No doubt if Méconille didn't kill me, he'd increase the dizziness and the storms and the whistling train in my head, by messing around in my mystery, in the inside. I was using it to take my mind off my agony. I didn't trust him at all to relieve my pain. You just had to look at him. First of all he was never without a pair of glasses plus a pince-nez, he had a beard bigger than his face, a tunic much too small for him (he couldn't separate his arms from his body), his hands were covered with hair right up to his fingernails, and his puttees splayed out, spiraling far behind his heels. In short everything that was filthy and annoying, that was Méconille. So no decision was made, and he shot me a dirty look the next morning when he did his rounds. So I was left to suffer in suspense, and then one morning L'Espinasse asked me very sweetly what my regimental number was. I gave her a number at random. It was none of her business. I'd let myself be identified, I decided, as late as possible. And the next day very early I was given ether. For horrible sensations, I was already spoiled, but L'Espinasse gave me a real treat, she pressed the anesthetic funnel firmly down over my nose with both arms. She was strong.

At first I had a high old time of it. I swear, they gave me so much that I launched myself into her delirium mask with a kind of joy in the end. As for bells, the ether caused a real personal uproar, a surprise actually. I plunged into that orchestra, for I'd probably never hear it again, as if into the heart of a locomotive. Only I sensed it was still my own heart powering the violence. And I had qualms about that. You have a good courageous heart after all, Ferdinand, I said to myself... You shouldn't abuse it... That's not nice, it's cowardly what you're doing... You're taking advantage...

And so I wanted to climb back up to the surface of the noise and give the head of that brat L'Espinasse a real beating... But she held firm with the mask, I was in her embrace as they say, the cow... Oh, for something to haul myself up with... In her hands I beat on the clapper of that bell with all my strength... Now here, in my head... *Boom* in the back of my eyes, *bang* against my ear. I've almost surfaced... Red... on... white... She was gaining the upper hand, the bitch.

So. When I tell about the shock of waking up now... I can hear myself screaming, like this: "Darling!"

And again even louder: "My darling!"

So that's what I'd found in infinity. I was emerging from the shitty nothingness with a darling! But I'd never had a pretty boy. Never in my fucking life have I ever had a darling pretty boy, that's for sure. It was a wave of tenderness that rose up strong and that disgusted me to hear it. And at the same time I see flowers and the screen and then I puke bitter bile all over the pillow. I writhe. I tear at my arm. It took four of them at least, and men too, to hold me down. So I'm vomiting. And then the first thing I really recognize is my mother, and then my father, and then beyond them Mademoiselle L'Espinasse. Everything becomes blurred and floats like at the bottom of an aquarium and then it finally stands still and I can clearly hear my mother saying:

"Come now Ferdinand, calm down, my little one ..."

She was crying a little bit and I saw she was upset seeing me so uncomfortable. Still in the midst of my delirium I understand that my father is there too, a little ways away. He had put on his white tie and his best suit to come.

"They've done a good job of setting your arm Ferdinand," L'Espinasse said then. "Dr. Méconille is very happy with how your operation went—"

"Oh we're very grateful to you Mademoiselle," my mother says, barely letting her finish. "I can assure you that my son will be deeply grateful, to you too Mademoiselle, you are taking care of him so devotedly."

What's more they'd brought some gifts from Paris which they'd taken from their shop, more sacrifices. There had to be proof of our gratitude right away. My mother at the foot of the bed continued to be terribly upset by my puking, and by my insults, and my obscenities, and my father thought that for such an occasion I was being extremely indecent.

They must have found some military papers in my pocket

since my parents had been notified. That thought hit me in the middle of my brain like a block of ice.

There was nothing funny about it. They sat there for a good two or three hours watching me come to. And I wasn't at all keen on hearing them or understanding the situation. And then my mother started talking to me again. She was playing the tenderness card. I didn't reply. She disgusted me more than ever. I'd have happily beaten her up, when it came down to it. I had a thousand and one reasons, not all of them clear but full of hatred all the same. I had a bellyful of reasons. As for him, he didn't say much. As if he was on his guard. With his fried-fish eyes. There they were in the war which he'd talked about forever, there they were. They'd come from Paris specially to see me. They must have had to ask for a permit from the commissioner in Saint-Gaille. Right away they talked about the store, the awful troubles they were having, business wasn't going well at all. I couldn't listen very well because of the racket in my head, but I could hear enough. It didn't incline me toward indulgence. I kept looking at them. They were a sorry lot there at the foot of my bed, and yet still virgins.

"Shit," I said finally. "I have nothing to say to you, fuck off…"

"Oh, Ferdinand!" my mother replied, "how you make us suffer. Come now, you should be happy. Here you are, out of the war. True, you're wounded, but with your constitution you'll get better soon. The war will be over. You'll find a good position. Be sensible now, and you're sure to live to an old age. Your health is fundamentally sound, your parents are in good shape. You know how we've never indulged in excesses of any kind … You've always been well cared for at home … Here these ladies are good to you … We saw your doctor as we came up … He speaks very kindly about you …"

I stopped saying anything. Never have I seen or heard anything as disgusting as my father and mother. I pretended to fall asleep. They left, whimpering, to go to the train station.

"He's delirious, you know, he's delirious," L'Espinasse said to excuse me and to console them as she accompanied them out.

I could hear her in the hallway.

It wouldn't be long now. One misfortune is always followed by another. Barely an hour later someone announces Madame Onime the canteen lady, in person. She too comes murmuring to the foot of the bed. I act delirious. She's wearing a little hat with a bird on it, and a little veil, and a boa and a fur. Luxury. A handkerchief for her sorrow, but I could see her eyes clearly. I knew her. She starts asking questions. She keeps beating around the bush. I wonder at first how could she have understood? I'd already stopped thinking about it, and then I thought about it again. There was no explanation for our expedition or the way it had ended. Those things you just feel. She couldn't feel that, Onime, that cow.

"He's dead," I said simply. "He died bravely!" and that's all. She fell to her knees then.

"Oh, Ferdinand!" she said. "Oh, Ferdinand!"

She stood up as if to stagger forward and then she went back down on her knees. She sobbed full-face into my blankets. I mistrust her sort. And I was right to do so. Now she's crying again. Mademoiselle L'Espinasse was listening not far away, probably behind the screen. She appeared all tight-lipped.

"We mustn't tire the wounded, Madame, the doctor forbids it. The visit is over ..."

She got up then, Madame Onime, all of a sudden, very annoyed, very abrupt.

"Ferdinand," she said very loudly so everyone would hear her, "you haven't forgotten that at the barracks you left me an IOU for 322 francs ... When do you plan on settling it?"

"I don't know Madame ... I don't get anything here ..."

"Oh, you don't get anything! Well I'll write to your parents again. I did have your word of honor, I seem to remember, that you wouldn't rack up any more canteen debts!"

It was to disparage me that she was saying all that in the presence of L'Espinasse. And she adds:

"I think I passed your parents on my way here. Maybe I'll see them at the station."

Then she rushes off on the double to the stairway ... I count to a hundred and then to two hundred. Barely half an hour later my father returns ... all hoarse, overwhelmed.

"Look here, Ferdinand, you didn't tell us that there's one more problem we have to deal with. The canteen lady just came to the actual station platform demanding we pay your debt. A debt you've owed her since you left camp. And here we've spent our whole lives for nothing, looking after you at the cost of sacrifices you're only too well aware of! You bring us nothing but shame. But 300 francs ... With things the way they are we'll have to borrow—who knows, we'll bleed ourselves dry, and your mother will have to pawn her earrings again. I promised to pay your debt in a week—I'm a man of my word, I am! Do you even realize, Ferdinand, we're at war now? Do you even think about that? Our business is going down the drain—you know how much trouble we're having ... I don't even know if I'll keep my place at La Coccinelle."

He had tears in his eyes ... But L'Espinasse intervened once more, urging him to treat me gently. He went out apologizing, muttering. They must all have run into each other at the station. Night fell.

It must have been around eleven o'clock that same night when L'Espinasse went out of her way to let me know that the next day I'd be transferred to a common room with the others, because more wounded men would be arriving. Yesterday I was really doing better, blah blah blah, but she thought I needed another catheterization. That wasn't the time to whine, to stand my ground. I knew this game—she picked the largest catheter in the row. It scraped. She did it all alone. Instinctively, I said to myself that if I refused, my credit would go way down. I suspected there was something behind it all. The thing lasted a good ten minutes. I cried then for real and not from emotion.

So. The next morning they transport me to the Salle Saint-Gonzef. My bed was between Bébert and the Zouave Oscar. Of the latter I won't speak because he never stopped doing his business through the catheter for the entire three weeks he was next to me. He spoke of nothing else. It was dysentery that held him in its grip from head to toe and also a wound in his intestine. His belly was like a tank of jam. When it fermented too much it overflowed through the catheter and down below the bed. Then he'd say it did him good. He smiled at everyone. Beaming. That does me good, he says again, he was brimming over. He finally died beaming.

Bébert on my right, though, that was another matter. He came from Paris like me, but he was from the 70th, from the Porte Brancion bastion. Right away he opened up my horizons. When I told him the story of my life, he thought it had been hard.

"Me, I made a choice," he said to me. "I'm only nineteen and a half but I'm married, I made a choice."

I didn't understand that right away but I marveled at him. I thought I knew my way around pretty well but he was unsurpassed. At the moment he was wounded in the foot, on his left toe to be exact, a nice little bullet. He'd seen through L'Espinasse's game, and much worse.

"I can tell you things about that skirt that you'd never imagine on your own."

He gave me back my taste for curiosity, did Bébert. That was a good sign. Plus, my arm was able to support itself ever since Méconille had operated on it. I could jerk off with my left hand, I learned.

But as soon as I got up I was as unsteady on my feet as a bowling pin. I had to sit down every twenty feet. As for the bees in my ears, the din was unimaginable. It was so loud that I asked Bébert if he could hear anything. I learned to listen to his stories through my own racket but he had to keep talking louder and louder. Finally we had a good laugh about it.

"You're eighty years old," he said, "you're as deaf as my sweetheart Angèle's uncle, the old guy who's retired from the Navy."

Angèle was his whole family, his wife — a legitimate one what's more, he spoke of nothing but her. She was eighteen.

As for the other guys in the room, there were enough wounds for every taste, on every surface and at every depth, reservists for the most part but idiots all of them. Many did nothing but enter and exit, to the earth or to heaven. At least one out of three rattled as he breathed. There were maybe twenty-five of us in all in the Salle Saint-Gonzef, but that night at ten o'clock I saw at least a hundred, then I rolled over on my bed and tried to keep my mouth shut so as not to wake the others. I was wracked by bizarre hallucinations. The next day I asked Bébert if he hadn't seen L'Espinasse come near my dick sometimes on purpose to jerk me off whenever I blacked out. No, he said. He was careful. But still I knew I wasn't just seeing things. Time passes. I end up seeing what's good about L'Espinasse. I stay with it. Her greenish teeth didn't frighten me at first, especially since she had magnificent arms, it must be said, very plump. I told myself her thighs must be beautiful too. I'd fuck her. I forced myself to get excited. One time, even though it was night, I was less delirious. She took advantage of the gas being turned down low to come say goodnight to me alone. It was nicely said ... She didn't put her

27

hand under my balls but I was expecting her to. It was becoming poetic, heartstrings were plucked. Even Bébert noticed.

"If you like, since she's so inclined, you can fuck the daylight out of the old gal, but I have to warn you, stay out of it if an amputee appears in this hellhole, since then the wind will turn and you'll be ditched in the blink of an eye. I'm not saying anything but you've been warned ..."

He knew things you wouldn't believe, that kid Bébert ... Fine. Two more weeks pass. We didn't go out, we didn't know what was going on outside but we must have retreated, the front was getting closer. Meaning we could hear the cannons even more from where we were lying, in a room over the courtyard. There were also enemy planes regularly around noon, not too bad really, three bombs at most. The ladies trembled in the toilets and their voices changed. There's a special kind of bravura in the gals. Méconille would simply hightail it to the staircase. He'd come back later ...

"It seems to me the planes are coming much more often," he remarked.

That annoyed him.

From my father, perfectly written postcards in perfect style. He urged patience on me, he predicted imminent peace, he talked about their hardships, their store on the passage des Bérésinas, the inexplicable nastiness of the neighbors, the additional work he was doing at La Coccinelle to compensate for the men away fighting.

"We paid your canteen lady, don't start up again where you are now, debts always lead to dishonor."

However he congratulated me at length on my courage. He surprised me a lot with the courage. He didn't know what it was, nor did I. In short he made me anxious. Even if I was in the process of dissolving into a fucking morass, so bad it was almost inconceivable, my father's missives held my attention, at bottom, by their tone. Even if we just had ten minutes left to live, we'd still look for the tender emotion of times gone by. In my father's letters my whole shitty dead childhood was there. I didn't miss any of it, it was a stinking pile of shit, full of anxiety, a horror, but it was still my little kid's rotten past he laid bare in the censored cards, with well-balanced, well-written phrases.

From where I was now I'd have liked, if I was dying, to have a music more my own, more alive, to help me pass away. The cruelest thing in this whole shitty situation was that I didn't like the music of my father's sentences. Dead, I think I'd rise up again just to puke over his sentences. You can't change the way you are. You can croak anytime, it's all the things that come before it that take away death's poetry—all the butcheries, the manglings, the jabberings, the torturations that come before the last gasp. So you have to be either very quick or very rich. When L'Espinasse came to feel me up at night I almost sobbed into her arms twice. I held it in. It was my father's fault with his postcards. Because I can boast about it now—when I'm alone I'm pretty brave.

You're probably dying to find out about the town of Peurdu-sur-la-Lys. Three more weeks went by before I could get up and was allowed to go out into the street. In fact I had my own anxieties too. I said nothing to Bébert. I think I sensed he had his own share of anxiety. My only protection was L'Espinasse when it came down to it. Méconille didn't count, she was the rich one who supported the hospital.

The priest came by every day. He too hovered around human meat, but he wasn't hard to please. A confession from time to time and he was happy. He gleamed. I went to confession. Of course I said nothing, minor things. I wasn't a total idiot. Bébert confessed too.

Méconille though was a much nastier sort, he couldn't wait

to extract the bullet. He peered inside my mouth and ear every morning, squinting through optics of all sizes.

"You'll have to have courage Ferdinand to have that taken out … Otherwise your ear is a goner … and possibly your head too …"

I had to act stupid, to resist without annoying him too much. Bébert, seeing me fight with Méconille, cracked up. The L'Espinasse broad, standing a little ways back, encouraged me to resist, but not too overtly. She looked as if it made her wet to see me resisting Méconille. She came by that night and, acting as if nothing was happening, gave my cock a good warm-up. When it came down to it she was my only protection, but still, as Bébert said, you shouldn't count on her too much. You're telling me. L'Espinasse was in so tight with the general staff that she could, apparently, recommend me for six months' sick leave and she'd never be refused.

But nothing was settled yet. One morning I see a four-star general coming in to the room, preceded by L'Espinasse herself. From the look they both had, I feel something bad is on the way.

Ferdinand, I say to myself, there's the enemy, for real, the enemy of your poor ass and of your everything. Look at the mug on that general … If you don't get him he'll get you, wherever you are, I say to myself under my breath. That's what separates me from the masses. Now, there's nothing but instinct that speaks to me and that's never wrong. You can give me a song and dance, you can mess with me, serve it up to me on a platter, sing me an opera, put bells on, even give me an ass made satin-smooth by the angels of paradise. My mind is firm, I dig my heel in deep, Mont Blanc on wheels wouldn't make me budge an inch. Instinct is never wrong about the ugliness of mankind. No more laughing. You count your bullets. It's funny.

So that mug comes over to my bed. He sits down and opens

his overstuffed briefcase. Bébert was listening too to see how I was going to deal with him. L'Espinasse introduces me.

"Commander Récumel, official examiner for the court martial of the 92nd Army Corps, is here to investigate the circumstances in which you fell with your convoy, Ferdinand.[*] It was a trap, wasn't it, Ferdinand, like you told me ... Spies that tracked you on the way and on ..."

She was throwing me a line, the doll. She was arming me so to speak. Récumel's face was not sweetness and light. I'd known lots of mugs of all ranks who even when they're poking their noses into other people's business, a rat would have thought twice before taking a bite. But Commander Récumel surpassed my experience of repulsive mugs. First of all he had no cheeks. He just had hollows everywhere like a dead man, and then just a little bit of yellow skin, taut and hairy and see-through. Under that void, there was surely nothing but spite. Deep inside the emptiness of his eye sockets, eyes so intense that nothing else counted. Covetous eyes, a little Andalusian. No hair either, white light in its place. Looking at that one—even before he says anything, Ferdinand, I tell myself again, you don't need to look any further. Surely there's no one more scoundrelly, more frightening in the entire French army, he's a special case, if this guy can find a way, they'll shoot you at dawn tomorrow.

So I had to listen to the questions he asked. Everything was written down, but what I noticed right away and what gave me hope is that he didn't know a thing about what he was saying. It was all made up. If I'd had any education, I could have spotted him as an ignoramus right then and there. He was rambling. I could sense he was talking crap, but I didn't see my chance of sticking it to him. I could have made all my comrades laugh. He

---

[*] Commander Recumel is described as a general earlier but the four stripes were worn at the time by "commanders" (squadron or battalion heads).

had no idea what happened with Le Drellière and the convoy. He wanted to act as if he knew. That's where he was a total idiot. These things can't be imagined, especially by the hard-hearted. You can sense that and then it's funny. So there's nothing to explain. I let L'Espinasse talk, and a lot like my father, that broad knew how to talk, she knew how to say nothing. He didn't dare interrupt her. She definitely had clout everywhere, she was a powerful one, I could have kissed her teeth. Still this sinister guy wanted my hide. He went back over everything. What was left of it, that is. He fidgeted on the little metal chair, his buttocks made noises like castanets he was so agitated. But his innuendos were so wide of the mark that it was laughable and even tiresome. I almost set him on the right track, I almost helped him out. He was annoying me with his blunders. He had no clue about the finer points of the War of Movement or of an independent cavalry. They should have sent him off with the dragoons first, to get a beating. Then when he came back he might have known, he might have learned a thing or two. Getting the picture is everything in life, even for killers.

"I see Corporal that you haven't remembered much about the precise orders you were given, not even the contents of a single one of the messages that must have been sent to you along the way. I count a dozen dispatches. They kept coming ... from the moment you left the ... station up to the time when events became so rapid, so inexplicable, that is, four days later when your convoy was forced to shelter at the Comté farm, exactly half a mile from the river, and was completely annihilated by enemy shells ... after the last about-face and a number of variations on the itinerary determined by your superiors, changes which remain entirely inexplicable and frankly astonishing since you were then twenty-six miles north of the main road. Can you however make an effort, one more time, since you are now the only survivor of this grotesque saga … The only semi-lucid one that is, since Krumenoy, the cavalryman from the 2nd squadron, who was found near the Montluc hospital, hasn't regained the use of speech for going on two months now."

I decided to have no more power of speech than Krumenoy. I kept silent. We had nothing in common. First, he spoke slightly elegantly like my father. That was enough. Bébert was quietly laughing his head off on his cot. My inquisitor turned to him and gave him a dirty look, which didn't bring Bébert any luck. I'll tell about that later … I thought, by not talking, what could he charge me with in the end? Desertion, faced with the enemy? Abandoning my post? Something sweet …

"Fine," he said at last, "I'll inform them," and he got up.

I never saw that guy again, but I often thought about him. His job was a funny one. L'Espinasse was my savior. You're a lucky guy, everyone said, but really they were jealous, the guys on the cots all around, half-starved and moaning and bleeding as they were. Ferdinand, I said to myself, if that asshole tries to bring you down you have to save yourself. Find yourself an alibi, your happiness is making people jealous …

I could see that the *bicot* corporal, the one missing an eye, was becoming reckless he wanted to fuck the broad so much.

Two more weeks go by. I can stand up for a bit. I could just hear with one ear, in the other it was like I was in a forge, but that was OK, I wanted to go out. Bébert wanted to go out too to take stock of things. That makes two of us asking permission from Mademoiselle L'Espinasse! That same night she came back again to my prick, with the gas down low, L'Espinasse, to my bedside. She breathed into my nose. It was a question of life or death I was well aware. I mustered my courage. Now or never. I catch hold of her mouth, both lips, I suck her teeth, between her teeth, her gums with the tip of my tongue. That tickled her. She was happy.

"Ferdinand," she murmured, "Ferdinand do you love me a little …?"

I couldn't speak loudly, the others were just pretending to snore. They were jerking off. Outside through the darkness, *boom boom*, there was a repeating cannon twelve miles away, maybe closer. I kissed her arm for a change. I put two of her fingers in my mouth, her other hand on my zozo. I wanted the bitch to care for me. I went back to sucking her mouth. I'd have put my tongue in her asshole, I would have done anything, guzzled her menstruation, so that jerk from the War Council would be screwed. But she wasn't fooled, that little lady.

"You were afraid before, weren't you Ferdinand? Of the Commander … Your explanations weren't making much sense …"

I kept mum. I didn't really understand her anymore … I stammered to cover it up. She liked it that I was afraid. She came, the cow. She was rubbing against my prick. She had a powerful Flemish ass. It was as if she'd driven herself straight into me she came so hard, on her knees. It was prayer.

"Tomorrow morning you'll go to the first Mass, Ferdinand, and you'll pray to God and give Him thanks for the protection He grants you and for the improvement of your health. Good night."

It was over—she had come, and she left. The other cripples were having a ball. As sensation it was all a cup-and-ball game. Twelve balls. Two balls. Zero ball … Bullseye …

I kept an eye out the next day. Nothing came from the War Council. I fished for hints without seeming to from the bedridden guys who had memories of the campaign.

"Have you ever seen anyone executed?" I ask the artilleryman, the one who had shrapnel in his lung, and the tip of his tongue blown off.

"Well I shaw one at ze shtake in Shizonne, dey aim zo bad it took tree times … Ain't funny."

That wasn't helping.

"Lucky a offisher," he went on, "put tree more bullets in hish head."

With that I could easily picture it. I wondered if they'd bring me to Romanches to shoot me or if they'd do it in Peurdu itself. Anything can happen.

I spent the night between the roar ringing in my ears, a fever, and my thoughts of the future. A little longer and I'd have gone to find the L'Espinasse dame … and also shit, I'd said I wouldn't lose, I didn't want to lose. Two more days, three more nights. Still nothing from the Council. They hadn't yet said anything to me about the regiment's cash box which had been busted open too, melted in the explosion, and yet that was the most serious thing they could pin on me, that bunch of world-class bastards whom I wouldn't even have thought of till the last moment. Even feverish at night I could all the same manage to prepare idiotic answers for them. Still nothing. I watched the dawn the next morning, the very gray day of the North in very clean windows above steep Flemish roofs, gleaming with rain. I saw all that, I saw life returning.

What with the sinister commander, and Méconille who was wondering if he'd lose me before finding my bullet, and the chaplain who came twice a day to give me eternity, and the fucking buzzing that made my whole middle ear tremble, it was a marvelous life, a life of torture, a torment that took away all my sleep or almost. Never, this went without saying, would I live the life of others, the life of all those idiots who think it's a matter of course, sleep and silence, and that once you have them they're there for good. I saw the door open for the nurse on duty three, four times and then one morning without any announcement, a *bicot* whose leg was bashed in by a howitzer just above the knee arrived from the train.

"Watch your skirt," Bébert warned, "you're going to have a laugh."

In fact, the instant the *bicot* entered the Salle Saint-Gonzef, she scarcely gave me a second look. You had to see how she went whispering around his bed, it was like she was trading a bone for a leg of lamb. Right away she catheterized the *bicot* with the extra-large catheter which I knew so well. He groaned behind the screen. They sure like to play us like a flute. Already the next morning the doctor operated on his thigh, a nice little amputation. After that she never left him. I'll catheterize you. I was as you'd say very jealous. Bébert made fun of me. I'll catheterize you again. He was sick as a dog, the *bicot*. They surrounded him with a screen. Then Bébert told me more. I didn't want to believe him, even though I'd seen things in my day. I tell myself Bébert's having me on. That got me up to go see for myself. Méconille didn't see anything—Bébert or me, that is. The others didn't have a clue. The Arab didn't hang around behind his screen, two days later he was so sick they took him down to the lazaretto.

He must have been jerked off a good ten times on the last day, well-catheterized too and not for fun, by the head lady behind the screen. Now in short he was dead, and they could take him down. I could have made a scandal with what I knew but that wouldn't have done me any good. Since I could get up now and go to the end of the room, I plucked up my courage. I looked her straight in the eyes, that L'Espinasse broad.

"Could I go into town today after lunch?" I asked.

"But Ferdinand you're not thinking, you can barely stand up."

"It's nothing," I said. "Bébert will support me if I stumble."

It was brazen of me. Especially what with the whole court martial thing, I shouldn't have gone out at all. They could come collect me any minute.

Outings from the hospital were exceptions, favors — I couldn't chicken out.

I said what I said ...

"I want to go out for five hours."

She looked me up and down, the floozy, she curled her lip over her teeth for an instant, and I say to myself she's going to bite. Not at all.

"That's fine Ferdinand, you can go out but with Bébert, but don't go into the main street, you'd definitely meet the guards from HQ and I'd be blamed for sure and you'd go straight to prison, I warn you."

I didn't even say Thank you.

"Bébert, at two o'clock we beat it, but the other cripples can't find out that we've gone jaunting off. In the ward we'll say we're going to a specialist and you're taking me to support my arm."

"OK!" he said and we laughed hard about the special specialist who'd come just to see me and who we were going to visit at the other end of the garrison.

Still they're cunning, the wounded. For now they believed our tale. Everything's OK. At two o'clock we go out into the street. It was a narrow alleyway. But the cool wind felt good.

"It's the end of winter Bébert," I say. "Hope soon! One bout of spring and, I warn you, my head will be buzzing more than ever!"

Bébert was always suspicious. We couldn't run into any of the top brass. He didn't make a sound with his slippers as we went from one door to the other, taking shelter in a doorway for a little while. We looked at the gardens, the trees over the little brick walls. In the sky there were puffs of exploding shells and also puffy clouds all pink and pale. The doughboys we passed wore uniforms different from ours, all one color and less fancy. The fashion had already changed since we'd entered the Virginal Secours. Time passes so quickly. The pure air gave me a lot of dizzy spells but with Bébert supporting me I could still walk. On the pavement I was overcome with a desire to fucking roam around. I wasn't dead. That reminded me of the time when I hawked my engraved pieces for the store up and down the boulevard and it had ended so badly. Better not summon up memories, they'd spoil my day. It's incredible how few of them were funny.

Peurdu-sur-la-Lys's appearance was a riot. For us at least. The central square was like a real museum, all lined with pretty, perfectly preserved stone houses. A market with carrots, turnips, salt pork right in the center. A treat to look at. And earth-shattering trucks rattling everything, houses, markets, babes and soldiers with hands in their pockets and all kinds of weapons, gossiping behind the cannons, under the arcades, in little groups on the corners, in yellow and green, North Africans, Indians even, and legions of cars, whole fleets of autos ... It was all spinning around like in a circus. It was the heart of the town, everything left from there, bombs, carrots, and men setting off in all directions.

Others were returning looking crushed, filing by crestfallen, making a line of mud past the dragoons wearing all different colors in the square. We liked the whole spectacle, Bébert and I. After a while, we sat in the shade in a little dive, looking outside and drinking it all in.

Bébert wasn't a pleasant sight. At first glance, he didn't inspire confidence but the boy had depth.

At first, he was the one who paid. He had money.

"My wife is getting by, she's doing well," he said. "She has a job, I don't like to go without ..."

I understood. I'm not a complete idiot.

In this town everyone passed through the main square.

"I'm positive," I said to Bébert, "that if we stay here long enough we'll see Commander Récumel go by ..."

"Don't think about it," he says, "look at that skirt instead ..."

It's true she had cleavage ... but there were already two colonial troopers feeling her tits, one each.

"She's taken," I reply.

"You'll see my Angèle is twice as good when it comes to prettiness and everything. This one's a bitch dog," he announced loud enough for her to hear. "I wouldn't want her to polish my prick."

And he spat a big wad on the skirt's shoes, to prove it to me. So then she looks over to him, she stares at Bébert who goes on eyeing her with disgust. Suddenly the skirt broke out in a real smile, she ditched the two sergeants and came over to him, her expression all changed and charming.

"Watch out, you fat broad, you'll hurt my foot. Bring me two shots and clear off. I could put that bitch to work for me too but first I have to see Angèle ..."

And then behind the half curtain he scowled, looking out at the main square, and he didn't even glance at her, the gal, as if she didn't exist. But it seemed as if she kept trying to get him to spit again. He paid no attention. He was thinking.

I let him think. I was meditating a little too. I was trying to be up to the situation.

"See," he said after a good while, "the town's full of Englishmen! ...I'll write that to Angèle ... Now that I'm going out I'll get by ... If my foot keeps suppurating two or three months more, Angèle will make you laugh Ferdinand. You'll even be able to send your old folks some money orders ... I'll hand the slut over to you, I'll break her in for you ... I can't do any better ... I can even find another extra whore ... Bitches like L'Espinasse I don't believe in ... They're traitorous. Sadism I don't mind, but one day it turns against you, you can't keep them, but with Angèle I know where I'm at. You'll see how it pays ... It's like a hunting dog... You've seen hunts ..."

Yes I'd seen hunts but I preferred not to talk about them. In short we had a good time. The shot went to Bébert's head. He was bullshitting a little, boasting. That was his weakness. He had two, then a third. The skirt didn't want him to pay for the last two rounds. All on her.

"Don't step on my foot you slut," he replied in thanks.

He pinched her ass, but hard, and then all over under her skirt so she grimaced. For so long that she turned pale. We got up and left.

"Don't turn around," Bébert told me.

I was starting to stand on my own. There were some civilians in the café along with soldiers and cops in civilian clothes probably, and a lot of them too—all kinds: merchants, farmers, Belgian grenadiers, and British sailors. A big player piano was rapping out music with its cymbal-machine gun. Along with the cannon fire in the sky, it was funny. That's how I heard "Tipperary" for the first time. It was almost night now. We had to go home keeping close to the houses. Not too quickly since we couldn't, either of us.

"If my foot suppurates for just two more months Ferdinand," Bébert went on, "just two months, listen, just with Angèle, you understand, just with her, I'll make a fortune ..."

The talk went on like that. Except we couldn't show ourselves. In principle there shouldn't have been anyone in the streets. While we took cover a cop patrol went by and then a whole squadron of gendarmes and then English policemen with billy clubs and armbands. Fortunately a detachment of engineers saved us, without it I think we'd have been done for. Pontonniers with their boats upside down on gun carriages. A real bazaar—chains, routers, planes, pans—enough that we could get mixed up in all their equipment, we were just two more instruments. Now we're both limping along in the horde moving in the direction of our street fortunately. Just at the corner we break off. In three lurching swerves we reach the little door to the Virginal Secours, the one that led to the lazaretto below. I didn't much like going in that way.

"It's nothing," Bébert asserts, "but we won't go in together, I'll go in through the garden, I can't go down stairs with my foot. You go down."

So I open the gate. I don't make a sound. I push very quietly —it creaks a little all the same. I stand still for a minute peering into the dark. There's another door further on, a band of light underneath. I walk over. I'm still careful no one hears me. Because of the ringing in my ears I never really know how much noise I make when I walk, or how much I don't make. I walk over all the same. There's the noise of a nail groaning in a board, and also wood creaking a little, being forced ... I say to myself that's where they're closing up a coffin. It must be the *bicot* they're boxing up. Tomorrow will be the burial. That didn't take long. They were probably in a hurry to get rid of the *bicot* because of the gangrene stench that already stank strongly through the phenolic acid. There were others in the lazaretto on stretchers that would go after him, who didn't stink so much. Still, where I was behind the door I could also hear the person murmuring words and it wasn't the voice of fat Émilien, the cabinetmaker everyone in the house knew, who was a souse, always a little drunk, his voice idem. It was a prayer then, in Latin. Maybe a nun who's come to say the rosary at the same time?

I'm intrigued. I hesitate for a second. If I don't look I'll see nothing. Above the partition, you just had to raise yourself up to peer into the little recess. I looked for a stool and finally I just climbed onto some empty boxes. They must have heard me ... I look. I could also hear echoing cannon fire booming through the windowpanes, it resounded all through the basement. I keep looking. Then be brave. It's funny, I didn't dare say it but I'd suspected it a little. It was L'Espinasse's voice I'd thought I'd heard speaking Latin. And she was busy. It was as if her whole life was in that box she was working so hard to open. With the cold chisel she was forcing it open, that was the creaking, especially since Émilien had sealed the coffin.

She was using both hands, and she was hurting herself. In the candlelight I couldn't see her head clearly, especially since she was leaning against the lid with her veil over everything. The stench didn't bother her. It did me. I don't try to understand but all of a sudden I sense I'm invading intimacy, real intimacy. I take advantage of the situation. I tap a little on the partition. She raises her head, sees me fully from her candle not two yards away.

Then she makes me afraid. I recoil a little. It's not a grimace on her face, it was something else, her mouth like a huge pale wound all salivating, trembling.

"Bleed, you hag," I say to her, "bleed, you bitch!"

I swore at her like that because I didn't know what to say. And because that's what came from inside, and it wasn't the time to make sense. I'm staggering. I push open the door of the boxroom.

"Bleed then, bleed!"

It was a stupid thing to say but I couldn't say anything else. Then she comes over to me and with all her face she kisses me and sucks me as if I were dead too and with both her arms she held me and trembled too. And then she became heavy all of a sudden and let go completely and she slid to the floor and I held her up.

She'd almost fainted.

"Aline," I say, "Aline!"

That was her first name which I'd heard in the rooms. She slowly got back up on her feet.

"I'm going upstairs," I say.

"That's right Ferdinand, I'll see you tomorrow. Till tomorrow. I'm better. You're nice Ferdinand, I like you …"

She went out into the street. She was almost the same as usual. But upstairs, Bébert was worried.

"I thought you'd gotten nabbed by the concierge," he says.

He had his doubts. I wasn't going to say anything, nothing, not to him or to the others. People have to be strong so as not to cause harm and also first of all it could be of use to me, and then it was of use to me.

I didn't believe much in new days. Every morning I was more tired than the day before from being awakened during the night twenty, thirty times by all the buzzing. Those kinds of fatigue have no name, the ones that stem from anxiety. You know very well you have to sleep to become a man like all the others again. You're also too tired to have the nerve to kill yourself. Everything is exhaustion. Every morning, when his bandage was changed, Cascade was content, his foot was not getting better.* Soon he would lose two toes, caries again. He wasn't supposed to walk, even in slippers, but the rot earned him special privileges from Mademoiselle L'Espinasse ... He never told me any particulars. He was on his guard with me too despite everything.

"What's your real name after all, nice tits?" he asked the barmaid, the second time we went back.

"Amandine Destinée Vandercotte."

"Say that's a nice name," Cascade remarked as if it delighted him. "You've worked here a long time?"

"Two years."

"So you know everything in the town? The people? Do you know L'Espinasse too? Do you go down on women?"

"Yes," she said, "and you?"

"I'll tell you after I've given your ass a pounding, and not

---

* The wounded man who before had been called Bébert now becomes Cascade, probably because Céline has inserted new pages into the beginning of this section. Soon he'll be given a first name and last name. Several times he's called Bébert again, but the name Cascade is the one that predominates from now on. See the index of recurrent characters.

before, bitch! How nosy these kids are, and cowards too! It makes you think twice!"

He pretended to be unhappy, insulted. He was exaggerating to impress me. It's true that with Amandine Destinée he could do no wrong. Never had she seen anyone so impressive.

We would go back there every day after grub, at noon, to the Hyperbole café on the Place Majeure. We had our corner, our own table. We saw everything. We were not seen. Our outings from the Virginal Secours made a lot of people jealous. L'Espinasse made us promise that we'd tell the other little shits in the beds next to ours that it was for electrotherapy that we went out every day.

"That's fine!" I said to that broad L'Espinasse.

Like Bébert, I was beginning to know how to talk. But still I kept my secret. Even Bébert I didn't trust. It's strange, the way he operated in everyday life. Never any noise. He preferred speaking with his hand in front of his mouth, except when he bawled out Destinée Amandine who chuckled with delight as he called her savage names that she'd never heard before, and on the sly he'd pinch her ass hard on her trips back and forth from the bar. He was a harsh one, Bébert. At least eight days in a row we went back to hide behind the half curtain at the Hyperbole. Bébert would watch the whole square, the movements of the troops, the people, the officers. He ogled the uniforms of all the armies. Amandine Destinée helped him.

"Over there on the corner in that sort of château is the English headquarters. The ones with the red bands on their kepis are the richest ones."

She knew this from their tips.

I'd listen to Cascade from daybreak on. He told me a little about Angèle, that she had mahogany-colored hair that was real and fell to her hips. As for coming, she could come twelve times in a row—that was nice. She'd get faint. As for blow jobs, no kidding, it was unbelievable, no joke …

"You'll see!"

He didn't overthink things, Bébert. A lot of things hadn't been gone over in his mind. I tried to get better. I had to. Life is even more awful when you can't get a hard-on anymore. It's just wrong.

"Tell me more about Angèle," I said in a low voice so as not to wake anyone up.

He told me how he'd fucked her the first time (in the ass), that it had hurt her at first, that she bawled for an hour.

The Zouave on the left, every morning I thought he was dead, he was so pale at daybreak. And then little by little he'd move and he'd start moaning again and his death only came in the second month …

I tried to tail L'Espinasse to see who she was jerking off now but there were so many wounded, several truckloads arrived full every day, that I couldn't find out. Peurdu-sur-la-Lys was an intense spot. They said there were at least four headquarters and twelve hospitals, three field hospitals, two war councils, twenty artillery lots between the Place Majeure and the second ramparts. In the large seminary they'd placed reserves from eleven surrounding villages. Mademoiselle L'Espinasse did a little to help those wretches too, so she said.

It was behind the big seminary in a courtyard that they shot people at dawn. One salvo, then a second a quarter of an hour later. About twice a week. From the Salle Saint-Gonzef I'd gradually been able to measure the frequency. It was almost always on Wednesday and Friday. Thursday was the market, those were other noises. Cascade knew too. He didn't like to talk about it much. Only he wanted to go there I was pretty sure. At least to see the place. Me too. The main thing was to go alone. We always went out together. Once it happened in a funny way that we surprised each other. There was an errand to do at the station. To get some medicine. Me, I wasn't supposed to go, ostensibly because it was too far and the package was too heavy to carry and also I had to be kept from falling a lot on the way. So Cascade leaves by himself. But I watched his face which wasn't entirely the way it usually looked. He was thinking out something for himself.

"I'm not going," I say to him.

Except while he was putting on his shoes with his back turned to me I swipe the chit from his greatcoat on the chair. He leaves. I let five minutes go by and then I ring for a nurse.

"Look, he left his chit. He'll never get his package."

And I leave presumably to catch up with him.

Now, I say to myself in the street, I can go and see what it's like behind the seminary …

I'm careful not to run into a cop. I reach the precise place where a kind of alley opens onto the street. At the far end is the wrought-iron gate to the courtyard. I go over. I lean down to look through the keyhole. You can see. It's a sort of garden with a lawn and the wall at the end, it's at least a hundred yards back, a sandstone wall not very high. Where do they tie them up? It's hard to picture. Finally it starts to dawn on you. I'd have liked to see the bullet traces. It's completely quiet. With the birdsong, it's spring next door. The birds whistle like bullets. They must stick in a new stake every time. I have to go to the station. I leave. I found him not far away, Cascade. He must have been going to the station very slowly. We said nothing. His face looked all stricken. Everyone's as brave as he can be. I give him back his chit.

"Go find the cashier," I say.

"Come with me," he says.

I was the one who supported him almost all the way to the

baggage claim. I realized later that he'd had a presentiment just from seeing me. On our way back we stopped by the Hyperbole. He said nothing, not one word to Destinée Amandine, nothing. She cried. We drank a whole liter of curaçao. I'm sure Cascade didn't sleep that night. The next morning he had a funny knowing look on his face. You shouldn't think he was sensitive. The proof is that he knew how to keep silent, for hours, thinking like that, looking straight in front of him. He had a nice enough face so far as I can judge people, with fine, regular features and rather large, idealistic eyes. But until he reached his golden years he was very severe with the broads and they knew instantly that he wasn't wrong, that he'd hit just the tone and was in the right. As for him, he took me for a nice lazy little idiot, corrupted by ordinary work. I'd told him everything, almost everything. I only held back the thing about the broad L'Espinasse, which was even more secret and which so to speak touched life itself.

In the meanwhile we didn't hear anything more about Commander Récumel from the Council. All we had to go on was the yard where the executions happened and where Cascade had had his premonition. The commander must not have gathered all the evidence of the affair against me yet. Often I seemed to be hearing him talk, but it was just a little delirium speaking, at night, when I still had a fever. I didn't say anything, I didn't want to be kept from going out. L'Espinasse didn't jerk me off anymore, she'd just come to kiss me around ten o'clock. She seemed a little calmer. The priest avoided talking to me now. He probably suspected. Even the lousy surgeon Méconille had become more polite. Bébert noticed all these little changes around us but he didn't really get it. Still he was gathering information, all the war talk in town. At the Hyperbole, as I said, in the shade of the café, there was a godawful racket, especially from the player piano. When everyone was shouting all at once it made a kind of silence in my ears. Noise against noise. Only then I tended to feel sick. The conflict in my head was just too strong.

"Come on Ferdinand," Bébert said to me, "you're getting pale. Come on, we'll go for a walk along the river, it'll do you good."

We went limping over there. We watched the shells bursting in the sky far away. Springtime had come back beyond the poplars. We returned to the Hyperbole to continue our task of observation. As a parade of troops, it was a real picture book and mostly happened around eight o'clock in the evening for the changing of the guard.

Then the regiments would stream in to the Place Majeure like flows of lava, from top to bottom, right to left. They would roll toward the arcades around the market square, would cling to the bistros and flow by the fountain, would drink up entire troughs among the big clusters of lamps wavering through the axles. Everything would have finally melted together so to speak on the Place Majeure if they'd pulverized things and bodies a little. That ended up happening, they told me, one time when the Bavarians crushed everything on the night of the bombing on November 24th.

Then everything stopped gravitating around the Place Majeure and the Belgian troops gutted the Zeelanders with a single blow: forty-three bombs fell. Ten dead.

Three colonels were taken playing poker right in the priest's garden. I can't vouch for it, I didn't see any of it, I was just told about it. It was even rowdier and more boisterous at the Hyperbole when Cascade and I went there later. It must be said, the great sorrow in Peurdu-sur-la-Lys for the people who just spent two hours there, and there were more and more men on the Place Majeure, wasn't that there wasn't enough alcohol, or enough different kinds, no, it was the women. Amandine Destinée was the only barmaid we knew, and she only liked Cascade—that was obvious, it was a case of love at first sight. The other poor fucks, even if they came for her from Ypres, from Liège the heroic, or from Alaska, she scorned even their smell. There was no brothel, all the orders prohibited them, and violators were prosecuted, locked up, expelled by all four police forces.

They'd jerk off then as soon as they'd drunk and slept a little, they'd fuck allies in the ass too maybe, though at the time where we were that wasn't very widespread. In short, from Cascade's point of view, all this around us meant a lot of money almost for the taking. Angèle had to come there, that was his opinion. I objected, I must say, to my honor. Up to the end I resisted, because we'd already had enough of fate and dangers and threats. Despite the fact that he'd gotten married and they were very much husband and wife with Republican papers, still if Angèle got nabbed getting fucked here in Peurdu-sur-la-Lys at the exchange rate, even with his rotten foot Cascade wouldn't be exempt from having to go in the blink of an eye, or even sooner, to add to the numbers on the front line of the 70th ... Anyway, I preferred not to talk about the premonition. We understood each other. But there was nothing for it. It was as if he was obsessed, Cascade, under the spell of his downfall. He didn't stop until she got her pass. So now one morning without warning he lands Angèle in the Salle Saint-Gonzef. He hadn't lied, she was a born turn-on. She set your prick on fire at first glance, first gesture. It went much deeper, to the heart so to speak, and even to the furthest core which isn't very deep at all, since it's only separated from death by three trembling peels of life, but they tremble so much, so intensely and so strongly that you can't stop yourself from saying yes, yes.

Wherever we were placed, and me especially, if I compare myself to the others, in the bottom of that fishbowl of pain, she had to really hold out her biology to me, that babe Angèle, for me to be able to get it up again. She gave me the eye openly the minute she saw me and she encouraged me. It didn't bother Cascade.

"See Ferdinand I didn't lie, when she leaves look at her ass, when she goes off to the boys she'll provoke mutinies, I told you so, she sets you on fire ... Go on kid. Go find the arcades ... the Hyperbole café. Ask the maid Destinée, I told her about you. You'll stay with her ... I'll come get you in the afternoon with my buddy. Go and get your pass signed at the station ... Don't go out before I tell you to ... I have my ideas ... Get your papers in order ... Don't talk to anyone ... If they question you, cry a little, say your husband is very sick ... That's even true. You understand me ... now beat it ..."

I couldn't get over Angèle, doddering as I was I'd have sucked the inside of her thighs. I'd have paid anything if I'd had money. He was watching me, Cascade. He was enjoying himself.

"Don't get too excited, Loulou.* If you're still my buddy when you get hard again I'll let you fuck that dish and I want her to come, I want her to be as excited as she'd be for an officer—you see—I can't do more than that."

Small, very skimpy blouses were the fashion that summer. I thought of hers, and a sort of dreamlike veil with tits appeared before my eyes and then I was again in the grips of a huge thundering buzzing sound, and then I had to go throw up in the toilet because of the vertigo that overwhelmed me whenever I got worked up for too long.

We went out as usual. At the Hyperbole, Destinée was there as always among the soldiers—and Angèle too, drinking anisette with some Senegalese. Cascade didn't like that and he said to me:

"Since this is the first time, I don't want to shame her in front of my little extra, but if she mingles with guys right and left I'll

---

* Loulou: Familiar nickname for Louis Destouches; Céline also uses it once in *Death on the Installment Plan.*

pinch her in the fat of her ass ... I'll teach her to be promiscuous. See here, little wife," he said to her, "you've been acting a little weird since I've been wounded ... You better believe you're not in Paris anymore. I'm here and you'll go where I tell you and nowhere else ..."

Angèle wasn't too happy with what he said, that was obvious. I felt sorry for her. It's true that she seemed a little edgy.

"You'll see — Ferdinand won't have a high opinion of you anymore, but you only have to ask him, I've sung him all your praises. Show Ferdinand your snatch, go on show it I tell you!"

She wasn't happy at all was Angèle, not at all. She didn't want to. He was a violent one in those situations.

"Show him, or I'll hit you across the face with my cane!"

The Destinée kid was standing behind Cascade. She didn't know how to act but she was afraid for Angèle.

She didn't give in an inch, Angèle. He thought better of it because of the scandal it would have caused. She looked him slowly up and down. He was deflated. The whole war was crushing us there too. Cascade couldn't beat up his wife anymore. She gave him a good look for a minute from top to bottom.

"You stink Cascade," she yelled, "you stink and you can fuck off and I came to tell you that right to your face and I can ditch you whenever I like ..."

That stung him, that must have been the first time anyone had called him a shit right to his face, in front of everyone, and his wife at that ...

"Shhh!" he hissed. "Shhh!" he said again. "You've had too much to drink Angèle, if you say one more word about it I'll fuck you up when we leave ..."

He'd pulled himself together.

This was happening in the little room in back but she screamed so loud that for a while I was still afraid. And now she went on, so that I'd learn a thing or two, but in a whisper, it was all an act. He was crushed. That was understandable. Finally we had some drinks, with her money. She was sniggering from seeing him so fearful.

"I scared you stiff didn't I, Cascade, I own you ... I'm sick of your sorry-ass face ..."

"You're not human Angèle. You're not human," he said.

He was gaping like a fish — he was afraid. He left the Hyperbole just as the patrol was passing, to go back to the hospital. Still, she slipped us a 100-franc note, and then right in front of Destinée:

"You're not going to fight," she told him. "Tomorrow," she went on, "I'm the one in charge."

None of that was really important because in the end everything dissolved into all sorts of terrors and illnesses. I'm telling it here because it's rather amusing. But Cascade was terrified.

"I'd never have thought she'd get like that, Ferdinand ... It's the foreigners who are leading her astray."

That was his idea. He went to bed with that idea. In the morning he was still talking about it.

Angèle had probably corrupted Destinée at the Hyperbole. They were sharing a room. And then she started having more diabolical ideas.

My head hurt so much that I couldn't go out every day. I was sorry about that. First of all, I hurt too much all over to think about her. L'Espinasse was watching me. She'd stopped kissing me at night. She'd stopped talking to me. The Zouave next to me, he died. One night he wasn't there anymore when I came back. That night was even worse than usual. I'd gotten used to him, the Zouave, to his disgusting ways, to everything. The fact that he'd gone, I was sure, would be the sign for something worse. Nothing else could happen but the worst.

And then you'll see I was wrong. We were on our guard, Cascade and me, about what the Angèle kid would do in town with her residence permit. No matter how much of a pimp he was, he had no more authority over her.

"You don't know what a woman can do in these kinds of situations. She's like a panther that's escaped from its cage, it doesn't obey anyone … It's the most idiotic thing I've ever done in my life to have her come here. I was thinking like I used to … I was seeing her like I used to … I don't know what they could have done to her …"

He was starting to realize.

"I'm sure she's whoring around with everyone. She'll get nabbed and then I'm sure she'll snitch on me … because I tell you she's become a snitch … And that's how they send her back to me from Paris despite the fact that I'd put her up at my sister's before I left. It's unbelievable. Just let me find her at it, I'll make her into a doormat for the cops, you hear me, a doormat just with the skin of Angèle's ass, I'll give her such a beating before I kick her out."

With both hands he was outlining a big square at my feet.

Except for the dying ones, all the other guys were having a good laugh hearing him rail against his girl. First of all they were sick of Cascade's stories, they didn't get them, they preferred cards over everything, and spitting too, and pissing drop by drop into their urinal while they waited for someone to write to them from their home front that everything was fine and that there would be peace soon. It was the cannon fire, and around July 15 it started getting closer and closer, that had become annoying. Often you had to speak loudly in the ward, very loudly to be heard, to call your cards. During the day the sky was burning so much that your eyes were still full of red when you closed them.

Fortunately our little street was very calm. To the right was the Lys flowing by not two minutes away. We followed the tow-path a little, and in that way we reached the other side of the ramparts, the one looking out on the countryside, the peaceful side of the fields in short. There were sheep on the peaceful side grazing in the lush greenery. We watched them, Cascade and I, feeding on the flowers. We sat down. We could almost not hear the cannon anymore. The water was calm, there was no more river traffic. The wind blew puffs through the poplar trees like little laughs. The only annoying thing was the birds whose cries sounded so much like bullets. We didn't talk much. Ever since I'd seen Angèle I told myself that Cascade was in at least as much danger as I was.

Troops weren't passing along the towpath. All the traffic was interrupted. The water lay black with water lilies on it. The sun goes by and nestles gladly into the dark—for no special reason, it's a sensitive one. I was beginning to put a little order into my buzzing—the trombones on one side, the organ only when I closed my eyes, the drum at each heartbeat. If I hadn't had so many fits of dizziness and nausea I'd have gotten used to it, but at night falling asleep was hard. You need joy, relaxation, aban-don. Those were things I could no longer lay claim to. Cascade had it easy, compared to me. I'd readily have both my feet rot if only my head could be left alone. He didn't understand that, one doesn't understand the obsessions of others. It's ridiculous, the peace of the fields for anyone whose ears are full of noise. Might as well be a musician for real. Or maybe have passions like L'Espinasse, since that takes up so much of yourself? Or be like the Chinese, who console themselves by torturing people.

I too should find a nice lunatic thing to make up for all the misery of being locked up forever in my head. Now I can never again just sit and do nothing with this racket in my head. I couldn't say if I was crazy or not, but I just needed to have a little fever for weird things to start happening to me. I no longer slept long enough to have clear thoughts that you can hold on to. I wasn't attached to any of them—and that's what saved me in a sense, if I can say so, because I'd probably have ended everything on the spot. I wouldn't have waited too long. I'd have let Méconille do what he liked.

"It's soothing, the countryside," Cascade said, looking at the fields. "It's soothing but it's treacherous too because of the cows. Me, I found my name in the woods. My name isn't really Cascade, or Gontran, my name is Julien Boisson."

He handed that to me like a confession. And then we left. He was anxious. On the way back we avoid going by the alleyway to the firing squad enclosure. We chose peaceful streets, streets with convents. But there too our minds didn't feel at peace, it was too calm. We break away, we choose the fate of walking in the middle of the street.

"Let's go and see what she's doing," he says.

For three days we hadn't dared go back to the Hyperbole. So we turn onto the street with the town hall on it and then the one that has a huge staircase fanning down to the middle of the central square. We stay there. We inspect the site first before we cross. We always had to steer clear of the pigs—our outings weren't entirely aboveboard. The Belgians especially were assholes. As policemen, no one's more swinish than them. They're crafty, they're cunning, they know all the intersections of two or three races.

On the Place Majeure there was traffic, the usual chaos, along with the umbrellas of the market which was held every day now, there was so much business. A little to the left was the most beautiful building, the one that had at least three floors made of sculpted stone, the British headquarters. You should have seen the kinds of automobiles and well-dressed guys that came out of there. The Prince of Wales came, apparently, every weekend. They also said they'd received the Crown Prince, who had come one Sunday to ask them not to shoot the cannon, so there could be three hours' peace to bury the dead. That gives you some idea.

Well who did we see? Not a hundred feet away from an English sentry? Wearing mourning from head to toe? We easily recognized her. Cascade paused for a minute. He thinks. He has understood.

"You see Ferdinand, she's turning tricks … I'm telling you she's doing the Englishmen …"

I wasn't an expert but that did seem to be Angèle's habit for the moment. Cascade's still thinking.

"If you bother her, full of herself as she is, you can expect anything Cascade! Me, I'm out of here—"

"Stay here. We'll take everything slowly. Or rather, say nothing except that I'm here. Go over by yourself and sing her your song."

It didn't go too badly. She was having a good laugh was Angèle. She'd already done three officers the night before, nothing but English guys.

"They're generous, they feel sorry for me."

That's what explained the veil, she had, so she said, already lost her poor father in the Somme and her husband was there in the hospital in Peurdu-sur-la-Lys. The husband was indeed Gontran Cascade and her false pass inspired confidence. So it was all aboveboard, and the British officers had had a French lesson, and with emotion too. Just the night before she'd made twelve pounds off of them.

"You didn't steal anything," I said.

"No, nothing, and they got a lot of pleasure, believe me, out of my sadness."

She had a good laugh with me and I took advantage of it to feel her up a little.

Cascade was waiting for us at the Hyperbole, as we'd planned, if I could settle things down. I didn't fail. I can't say if I seduced Angèle but she had more time for me than for her husband. She couldn't stand the apprentice whore, the barmaid Destinée — she was still staying in her room, though.

"Listen, your little whore," she said to Cascade suddenly, "couldn't you teach her to wash her slit before she goes to bed?"

I thought he was going to hit her across her face, but he'd already lost his manhood. Bébert was already leaving, off to meet his destiny, and it was as if he knew it.

"It won't bring you any luck Angèle what you're doing here, it won't bring you any luck, remember that, you picked up weird habits in Paris while I was away. You don't have the smarts to play the man Angèle, it'll go to your head, it'll be the death of you, even more than me … remember that."

He was speaking gently to her. He surprised me.

Before we left she slipped him in front of everyone another 100-franc note. There was enough for us both. I didn't ask my parents for anything anymore. We saw them again, my parents, we saw everything and everyone all of a sudden. It all came back like a violent gust from the past. I'll tell you why. One Sunday, L'Espinasse comes to the end of the room with a wide friendly smile directed at me. At first, since I was rubbing myself off a little under my bolster, I'm on my guard.

"Ferdinand," she says, "do you know what the great news is that I'm going to tell you?"

I say to myself that's it, they're court-martialing me sight unseen, right away.

"No? Marshal Joffre has just awarded you the Military Medal!"

So I emerge from my shelter.

"Your dear parents are coming tomorrow. They've been told too. Here's your magnificent citation—"

She read it out loud for everyone.

"Corporal Ferdinand has been mentioned in the army's dispatches for having 'single-handedly attempted to free his convoy by making it his mission to clear the road. When the convoy, surprised by artillery fire and enemy cavalry reinforcements, found itself under attack, Corporal Ferdinand, all by himself, charged a group of Bavarian lancers three times, managing, thanks to his heroism, to cover the retreat of three hundred of the convoy's walking wounded. Corporal Ferdinand was wounded in the course of his exploit.'"

That was me. Right away I say to myself, Ferdinand there's been a mistake. This is the time to take advantage of it. I can say right now that I didn't hesitate for a second.

Such reversals of things don't last. I don't know if there's a link, but the front facing Peurdu also moved that day: The Germans withdrew, a sudden reversal, they said. We almost stopped hearing the cannon. The other guys in the ward couldn't get over my sudden distinction. They were a little jealous, actually. Even Cascade was interested to a certain extent. I didn't tell him it was all a story, my medal—he wouldn't have believed me.

To be honest, starting from that moment things became both easy and odd. A great wave of imagination was rippling all around us. I had supreme courage—I let myself be carried along, believe me. I didn't give in to the surprise that would have kept me staying as idiotic as before, feasting on suffering and only suffering because that's all I knew from my education, from my good parents—and all their difficult, laborious, sweaty sufferings. I could have not believed in this funfair of imagination where I was invited to mount a steed all made of wood, all decked out in lies and velvet. I could have refused. I did not refuse.

Great, I said, the wind's blowing Ferdinand, rig your boat, leave the idiots in the shit, let yourself be carried along, don't believe in anything anymore. You're more than two-thirds broken but with the little bit that's left you can still have a good time, let yourself be lifted up by the favorable winds. Sleep or don't sleep, limp, blare, stagger, shout, foam at the mouth, drip pus, be feverish, crush and betray, nothing can bother you, it's just a question of the wind that's blowing, you'll never be as horrible or ridiculous as the rest of the world. Keep moving, that's all they're asking of you, you have the medal, it's great. In the battle of loudmouths you're finally winning in a big way, you have your special fanfare in your head, you're half-gangrened, you're rotten—that goes without saying—but you've seen battlefields where they don't decorate bastards and you're decorated, don't forget that or you're an ingrate, you're gross vomit, dribbling ass scrapings, you're not worth the paper they wipe you with.

I put the citation with Joffre's signature in my pocket and

started swaggering about. It was as if my luck were burying poor Cascade in the muck. He didn't even groan anymore.

"Good luck Gontran," I said to him. "You'll see how I'll own all the chicks, even L'Espinasse and the tribunal guys, and the bishop—listen, the way I'm feeling, I could fuck him right up the ass just if he doesn't talk to me when we're standing at attention."

My jokes didn't make Cascade laugh anymore.

"You're handsome Ferdinand, you're handsome," is all he said. "You should have yourself photographed."

"You're on," I said.

We were with my parents the same afternoon they arrived. My father was transformed. I had suddenly become someone. They were talking about my medal as if about the crossing of the Berezina. My mother had a little tear in her eye, a tremor in her voice. That disgusted me. I don't like my parents' emotions. We had more serious things to settle. My father was impressed by the artillery filing by in the streets. My mother kept saying how young the soldiers were and how well-seated the officers looked on their horses. They inspired confidence in her, the officers. My father also had a connection in Peurdu-sur-la-Lys, the insurance agent for La Coccinelle. We were invited to lunch to celebrate my Military Medal, and then even L'Espinasse as well—I was the pride of her hospital—and also Cascade too since he was always with me and then my mother wanted Angèle to come too since they were married. She didn't know anything about the situation. We couldn't explain it to her. They were leaving that same night. We looked for Angèle and found her at the corner of the English headquarters like the days before.

Cascade was just a wreck to tell the truth. He was melting down, especially when he saw Angèle. He wasn't even whining anymore. Destinée too took him for granted. She pushed back his chair so he'd be out of the way of the customers at the Hyperbole. It was a transformation of the man. I was swelling up thanks to the medal, whereas it was wearing him down, it came from the war and he didn't understand it. While I was gaining swagger, he was losing his, and it was as if he was giving in completely to misfortune.

"Fight it," I said, "you're under the spell of your girl Angèle and for now she's taking on filthy ways I admit. She's taking advantage of the situation we're in, but it won't last, you'll get her back when she gets hit hard. She'll still be happy for you to rein in her lies and you should do it right away."

"Listen I'm the one who'd happily give her up to the cops, that's how much I don't recognize myself anymore. Let them chuck her back to Paris and let her get fucked up the ass by her Negros. It's not about whether she stays or goes, it's simple, either I kill her or I get done in. It's fucked up, what war does to you, you can say what you like. I'm positive she has some jerk, unless she's a lezzie and I never had an inkling. I swear to you Ferdinand, Angèle's a monster."

Monsieur Harnache was the name of the insurance agent from La Coccinelle. As pretty houses go you couldn't do any better than his for comfort at the time. He was as friendly as possible. He showed us all around. It was old, my mother admired it a lot. She complimented him. She felt sorry for Madame Harnache for having to live so close to the front. And the cute little children, two boys, one girl, who sat at table with us. Monsieur Harnache had been rich forever, he took care of La Coccinelle to give himself a goal in life.

My mother admired him no end. In short he had everything going for him and so many good qualities. So rich, [a few illegible words] here with the troops so close to the front, with such lovely children around him, and, declared unfit for service because of his weak heart, he lived in such a big well kept-up house all furnished with "antiques" and with three maids and a cook, less than fifteen miles from the front, and so unassuming with us, so obliging, inviting us over for lunch on the first day, especially straightforward with Cascade, asking questions, admiring, almost venerating our wounds and my Military Medal, wearing a suit made of very expensive material, a very respectable collar, very high, impeccable, connected with the highest society in Peurdu-sur-la-Lys, knowing everyone, not at all proud despite everything, speaking English like a grammar book, decorating his house with filament lace, which my mother regarded as proof of the most refined taste, and writing my father letters almost as good as my father's, not entirely as good obviously, but still admirable, keeping—a rare thing already in those days—his hair in a brush cut, a severe cut that looks so proper and so perfectly masculine and respectable and inspiring such confidence for prospective policyholders. My mother, with her "woolen" leg as she called it, had difficulty climbing each floor, but she couldn't get enough of admiring everything in the home of Monsieur and Madame Harnache.

In front of the windows she paused to catch her breath, glanced into the street with the troops ebbing and flowing and stayed there for a moment, sorrowful, faced with this kind of carnival …

"You can still hear the cannon," she said.

And then she set off again to admire the next room where everything bore witness to the treasures of several generations of Harnaches. You could have shown her fish in a river instead of troops in the street, and she wouldn't have any more of a clue what was possessing them to keep moving one behind the other without respite in a flood of colors. My father felt obliged to give her vague, entirely imaginary explanations and to act the expert. Harnache himself politely explained the training of the [Hindu] troops …

"They always march two by two, apparently if one of the two comrades is hit by an enemy bullet the other won't survive him for long. Fact."

Then my mother would go into raptures. She'd get emotional.

"Careful Célestine," my father said, "where you put your foot behind you."

It was the very well-polished staircase of this ideal house.

"A veritable museum … What lovely things you have here Madame …" my mother kept congratulating her.

Madame Harnache was waiting down below next to the dining room with her three children. My father was afraid my mother would stumble in front of everyone. She was limping from having gone up and down all the other staircases at the train station and walking on the town pavements. My father grimaced whenever he thought of her shameful skinny legs. He was sure the others had also seen under her skirt as they were going upstairs. He looked like a lecher though, Harnache with his little cat mustache. He must have been fucking the maids. My father would sneak looks on the sly at the maids, when they handed out the hors-d'oeuvres. Plump, very buxom girls around twenty. When they went to the kitchen to carry the dishes they had to climb two steps, it showed their calves a little.

Mademoiselle L'Espinasse came a little late, apologizing profusely. At the entrance to the Place Majeure she had been held up by the parade of the Scottish troops that had gotten there the day before, their general gave them back their flag.

"How beautiful it was! What magnificent boys Madame! Almost children still, true, but with such superb freshness, bravery and endurance! … I'm certain that someday they'll do wonders and cause no end of trouble to those disgraceful Boches, those animals, those abominations!"

"Oh yes Madame indeed, we read atrocious details about

their cruelty in the papers. It's truly unbelievable! There must be some way to stop these things."

As for atrocities they spared our ears, Cascade's and mine. They didn't want to tell us everything they'd read in the papers. My mother thought there must surely be some ultimate recourse to someone very powerful to prevent the Germans from giving in to all their instincts. It couldn't be otherwise—and for once my father shared her opinion. If the Germans were allowed to permit themselves everything, then the world was different from what they'd always thought of it, [it was built on other principles and other ideas,] and what they thought had to remain their truth. Of course an ultimate recourse existed against the bestialities of war. You just had to do your duty as my father had always done in his own life. That was all. They couldn't conceive of this world of atrocity, of limitless torture. So they denied it. Merely envisioning it as a possible fact horrified them more than anything. They tucked into the appetizers heartily, they all got flushed spurring each other on to deny that nothing could be done against German atrocities.

"It won't last. All that's needed is an American intervention."

It was obvious to Cascade and me that Mademoiselle L'Espinasse was a little hesitant about getting as indignant as the others. She was watching us and we were very submissive. To tell the truth, they were all talking a bizarre language, the high talk of idiots.

The best thing is that Angèle finally arrived. My mother—who was always putting her foot in it—immediately congratulated her on her courage in joining her husband in the danger zone... Was she going to stay much longer... Was she authorized...

Angèle never stopped staring wide-eyed at my Military Medal, fixedly.

I could easily have fucked Angèle if I'd had a little sleep first and if I could have been sure of my safety for a day or two. The medal didn't give me any sleep but still it gave me a tiny bit of security. Except there was Cascade.

We got to the leg of lamb. That's when we stopped thinking for a while. I had three more helpings, my father too, Monsieur Harnache too, his wife two more, Mademoiselle L'Espinasse one and a half. My mother seeing me eat so much smiled at me tenderly.

"Well at least his appetite hasn't gone away," she remarked joyfully to everyone ...

They never talked about my ear, it was like the German atrocities—things that weren't acceptable, weren't solvable, were dubious, not respectable in short, which called into question the concept of the remediability of all things in this world. I was too sick, and I especially wasn't educated enough at the time to realize over my buzzing head the ignominy in their attitude toward my old hopes and all hopes, but I feel it on me at every gesture, I feel sick every time, like a leech slimy and heavy as shit, their enormous optimistic, inane, rotten idiocy, which despite everything they used to cover up the shame and the intense, extreme, bloody tortures shouting under the very windows of the room where we were stuffing our faces, and, in my own tragedy, all the degradations which they didn't even accept since acknowledging them would be to despair a little of the world and of life and they didn't want to despair of anything despite everything, even the war which was going on under Monsieur Harnache's windows with full battalions and which we could still hear rumbling from bombs echoing everywhere in all the windows of the house. About my arm they kept showering me with praise. It was a nice wound on which their optimism could be unleashed. On Cascade's foot too. Angèle said nothing, she'd put on almost no makeup.

"How nice the sweet little thing is," my mother whispered to me after the salad." [An illegible sentence]

There was a conspiracy at the table. Not only were they celebrating my bravery, they were boosting our morale, us wounded fighters.

It lasted a good two hours we ate so much. During dessert the chaplain, Canon Présure, stopped by to congratulate my parents. He spoke softly like a lady. He drank coffee as if he were drinking gold. He was sure of himself. My mother nodded her head as he offered his congratulations, my father too. They approved of everything. It came from heaven.

"You see, my dear friend, in the midst of the most terrible ordeals He permits His creatures to endure, the Lord still preserves immense pity for them, an infinite mercy. Their sufferings are His sufferings, their tears are His tears, their anguish is His anguish..."

I took on an idiotic and contrite look to agree with all the other words of the priest. I couldn't hear him well because of the uproar clamping my head like an almost impenetrable helmet of noise. It was only through these whistlings and as if through a door with a thousand echoes that his words reached me all oozing and venomous.

My mother's mouth gaped open a little, the priest said such elevated things. It was obvious that this was his custom, he never stopped saying elevated things, just as my mother never stopped being devoted and I never stopped buzzing and my father never stopped being honest. We all drank some more cognac and old cognac at that to celebrate the Military Medal again.

Cascade was downing Angèle's drinks to annoy her, he didn't even let her finish any. He gulped down all her drinks right under her nose. He thought it was funny. It was a kind of dance wherever we were in Monsieur Harnache's dining room, a dance of emotions. It came and went in the middle of my buzzings. Nothing was stable anymore. We were all drunk. Monsieur Harnache had taken off his tie. We drank some more coffee. We no longer listened much to the priest. Just my mother was still nodding her head, in front of his mouth, acknowledging the highest sentiments about the perils of war and the supernatural benevolence of the Good Lord.

Cascade was saying some harsh words in Angèle's ear. I couldn't hear very well but it was jarring.

"No I won't go ..." she was saying ... "no I won't go ..."

She was making him angry. He told me before we left that he'd liked fucking her in the toilet. She wouldn't go. Good.

"So I'll sing my piece!" he said.

And he got up from his chair. My father's face was flushed. The troops were going by, they never stopped, they flowed down the street like a heavy shower of metal, the cavalry, and then the artillery between the squadrons rattling, stumbling, wavering from one echo to the other. We were used to it.

"He has no idea!" Angèle said suddenly.

I saw her eyes clearly. It was defiance. The dark eyes she had and the blood-red provocative mouth and the eyebrows drawn severely over sweetness and attractiveness. You couldn't trust her. Cascade must not have realized it though.

"I'll sing if I want to and it's not you fish face who will make me shut up!"

"Just try," she said. "Try and see!"

I realize she was excited with the alcohol but still there were some things she shouldn't say, and she shouldn't act like that.

"What's that, what's that, bitch? You dare defy your husband in front of people here? You've let yourself be plowed by all the beefeaters ever since I sent for you to come see me here ... Who do you think you are? Why don't you tell these people how I found you whoring in the streets in the Passage du Caire and how without me you'd never have earned enough to show off your first shirt. Say one more word bitch and I'll bash in your face you whore! Fuck you didn't even deserve … you piece of filth!"

"Oh yes?" she says to him …

And in a lower voice, concentrating on each word which she must have prepared before she came:

"You say this Angèle kid must still be just as idiotic as she was before … That's what you're saying, is it? That she'll train one, two, three extra whores and all the bitches Monsieur brings with their rotten cunts, and every month a brat in the belly we have to pluck, with two or three venereal diseases for each one—that's expensive—and you think that the Angèle kid is going to honor all that, pay for the VD cures and the family drinks with her ass, with her ass again, always her ass … No sweetie, I'm fed up and you can fuck off—you're rotting, stay rotting. Go fuck yourself all alone, everyone for himself, that's my extra, evening edition!"

"Ferdinand!" he shouts. "I'm not saying one more word! You heard. I'll give you her guts …"

Monsieur Harnache was next to him, the priest, Mademoiselle L'Espinasse—everyone was speechless … He already had the cake knife in his hand. He couldn't have done much harm.

My mother heard these horrors. It was a shocking tone that she wasn't familiar with. They held Cascade back. He sat back down. He was shaking his head like a metronome. His wife was on the other side of the room fortunately. She didn't lower her eyes for that.

"Sing us something dear Cascade," Madame Harnache finally blurted out, too much of an idiot to have understood a thing: "I'll accompany you on the piano."

"Fine!" he said and went to the piano as firmly as if he were setting off to kill someone.

He didn't stop eyeing Angèle up and down. She was no longer agitated.

I know ... tralala tralala that you are pret—ty ...
Trala, trala.
That your big eyes full of sweetness, ness ness
Have captured my heart! ...
And that it's for life ... ife ... ife ...
I know ...

Then it was Angèle, provoking him again—she'd gotten up resolutely despite the priest who was trying to hold her down.

"Maybe there's one thing that you won't say, you disgusting lout, and it's that you've been married twice ... yes twice ... with fake papers the second time. His name is not Cascade, ladies and gentlemen ... not Cascade Gontran at all, plus he's a bigamist, yes a bigamist, and he got married with fake papers ... his first wife, she whores for him too, in Toulon, yes and she uses his real name ... that's his actual real name. Tell these ladies and gentlemen if that's not true ..."

"*You don't know? say you don't know!*" he kept singing.

The gathering didn't know what to do ... Angèle had gone over to insult him to his face: "Yes I know more ..."

"Well go on, spill it all, while you're at it, say everything you know since you're so smart. You'll see how you get out of this. You'll see how Julien ... he'll crush you, you rotten piece of shit. Go on, since you started go on—"

"I don't need your permission, not at all. I'll tell 'em loud and clear who bumped off the night guard at two in the morning on August 4th, at the Parc des Princes ... There are witnesses ... Léon Crossepoil ... the girl they call the Ballbreaker, they'll say so too ..."

"That's fine," he says. "I'll still sing. Listen you whorish piece of shit you'll see I won't stop singing, listen. Even if you got me guillotined, you hear me, guillotined even from the bottom of the bucket I'd still sing if I felt like it, just to piss you off. Listen.

I know tralala trala that you're pretty . . .
That your big eyes full of sweetness . . .
Have captured my heart . . .
And it's for life . . .
I know . . .

"You want another stanza! I'll give it to you, I'll give you all of them [a few illegible words]. All of them, so the shit'll come up and choke you. All of them, you hear me, I'm not scared of heights, you can tell them that. If you could only see what a puny thing a little cunt like you is to Cascade.

[. . . .
. . . .
. . . .
. . . .]

"I know all the stanzas, you hear me, and I can fuck you up the ass whenever I like."

"No, you won't fuck me up the ass, no you won't! You're not as brave as the lowest of all assholes. You're nothing but a complete incompetent, you're a loudmouth not even capable of controlling yourself like everyone else your age . . . You're more of a woman than I am, you're a bitch and don't say otherwise, more of a woman than I am!"

"What! what . . ." Cascade said then, all hesitant. "What are you saying?"

"I'm saying, I'm saying . . . that you're the one that shot yourself in the foot to come back behind the lines to piss me off ... Tell them it wasn't you ... Go on say it!" She added, pointing to him like a freak: "That's what he's like!" It was quite the spectacle.

He was tottering on his rotten foot, Cascade.

"I'll still sing for France," he said in a weary voice. "And listen," he went on, "you'll never shut me up, you hear me? The bitch who will wipe me out hasn't been born, she hasn't been born ... that's what I say. Go find a man if you want, you'll see if he'll shut me up. Is there one of you, you bunch of bastards, waiting in line to shut me up?"

No one answered of course. The priest was backing toward the door very slowly. The others didn't dare move. My mother was holding herself back from going over to calm Cascade down with maternal conformist words.

[..........................
....
.......................]

And then he stood there all swaying and proud near the piano. He sang rasping and off-key. It's strange that he didn't try to wrap things up with Angèle though she was almost next to him. I was noticing everything, as in a nightmare we could do nothing ourselves except suffer through everything ... He too was a nightmare, and Angèle too when it came down to it. It was good in a way. She recognized this.

"Yes, I'm telling you—you're the one who shot yourself. You told me so in a letter ... don't say you didn't write it."

"So what?" he asked.

"I sent your letter to the Colonel, yes I sent it. There, are you happy now? And now you'll shut your dirty trap, won't you, you'll shut it."

"No I won't shut it, no I'll never shut it you filthy rotten piece of shit … shut it yourself. I'd rather eat shit you hear me. I'd rather have my prick opened with a sardine can key than shut my trap because of you …"

"I'll accompany you, Monsieur Carcass," she says, Madame Harnache.

She hadn't understood a thing, she thought it was just a little quarrel …

Angèle sat down then next to my mother.

A cavalry regiment was passing by outside at that moment.

It was a real brass band I heard then. I thought it was Mademoiselle L'Espinasse joining in and playing the trumpet, a loud trumpet blow, and she even had a helmet, a helmet three times higher like the notes. It wasn't normal.

"Cascade," I said, "Cascade, I have such a … Long live France! Long live France!"

I collapsed. Everything stopped in the dining room, even Cascade's song. There was nothing but my buzzing noises throughout the house from top to bottom, and even further away, the whole cavalry charge hurtling down the street through the Place Majeure, one hundred and twenty big shells bombarding the market. Deep down I realized the delirium of things. For a minute I saw the convoy again, my own little convoy, I wanted to follow it. Le Drellière was gesturing to me, brave Le Drellière … He was doing what he could … me too … [I ran, ran … and then I fell.]

After so many years have passed, it's hard to remember things precisely. What people once said has almost turned into lies. Can't trust them. It's fucked up, the past, it dissolves into daydreams. It picks up little melodies on the way that you didn't ask for. The past comes back to you all made up, with tears and repentances wandering around. It's not serious. Then you have to ask for help quick from your prick, right away, to get back to yourself. The only way, the man's way. Have a huge hard-on but don't give in to jerking off. No. All the strength rises up to the brain, so they say. A bout of Puritanism, but a brief one. Then the past is fucked, it surrenders, for an instant, with all its colors, its darks, its brights, the gestures, even precise ones, of people—memory's taken all by surprise. It's a bastard, always drunk with forgetfulness the past, a real sly one that's vomiting over all your old affairs, which are already lined up, piled up that is, disgusting, at the very moaning end of days, in your own coffin, the dead hypocrite. But after all, you'll say, that's my affair. This is how things worked out, or rather came undone, in reality, after they'd revived me and I was back in the hospital.

Before that, I'd even taken my parents who didn't know what to think back to the station. I insisted on going there, swaying back and forth. With Cascade supporting me, who was still showing off on his two canes. The priest and L'Espinasse had gone their separate ways. Angèle was nowhere to be found. She'd beat it through the kitchen. My father especially was extremely upset by what he'd just seen and heard.

"Come on Clémence, hurry up," he urged my mother who

after sitting so long was limping almost as much as Cascade, "come quickly! There's only one train after this one, at eleven o'clock."

He was paler than any of us. He's the one who saw where things stood the quickest. I was still buzzing too much and Cascade had finished playing his role of the boy afraid of nothing. We were blocked every fifty feet by the troops. Finally we arrived in the nick of time to the whistle on the platform. Then it was just us two together. It was time to go back to the Virginal Secours on the double.

"Are we going?" I asked Cascade all the same.

"Of course," he says, "would you rather I go dancing instead ...?"

I say nothing. In the ward you could guess the news had spread just from seeing the guys under their blankets playing piquet. They weren't talking to each other much but they were trying not to ask us for news of the town, as they usually did when we came back, always idiotic things about the skirts, what we'd seen at the café, in the street, nice guys' questions in short. Nothing like that.

It's Antoine, the little male nurse from the Midi, the one with the plaster cast near the door who tipped me off as I was passing by to piss.

"You know the cops from the army corps came by at two to ask for Cascade, it was for some information they said ... did you hear?"

Right away I go back to Cascade and tell him. He says nothing.

Then he says: "It's OK."

Night came. They put out the gas.

I said to myself that's it, definitely—the cops already smell a rat, they're coming at dawn to pick him up. I heard the nine o'clock bells and then there was a cannon shot not very far away and then another, and then nothing. Except the usual din of trucks rolling by and then the cavalry and the huge whispering of the passing infantry soldiers' feet marching by the walls, a battalion passing. A whistle at the train station. I had to arrange all that in my head before I could go to sleep, I had to hang on tight with both hands to the pillow, trying to have willpower, to push away the anxiety that I'd never sleep again, to gather together my own noises, the whole percussion section in my ear, with all the noises outside and little by little I manage to last one hour, two hours, three unconscious, the way you lift an enormous weight and let it fall, only to falter again into another huge defeat. Then you snap, you can think of nothing but dying, you return to the burden of sleep like rabbits being tracked and hunted, into a trench, they pause there, stop moving, then start up again, full of hope. It's unbelievable the torture of the other side of sleep.

In the morning there was a lull. Echoes of shells bursting, that's all. The nurse brought the juice. I noticed that she didn't look at Cascade the way she usually did. She definitely knew things. She was a girl from the convent. L'Espinasse we didn't see anymore. She was busy in the operating room they said. I wondered to myself what role she might be playing in what was being prepared. After the juice Cascade went to the washroom and then he came back to play a round of piquet with Lardass as he was called, the heart patient who was one bed past the guy on the left. Lardass was not actually fat, his feet were swollen and he had a belly because of his heart condition and albumin levels. That's all. That had been keeping him in the sack for three months. When he suddenly deflated, we didn't recognize him. Then something happened. Cascade had won four games in a row with him, Cascade who usually never won. Camuset, the guy on crutches who saw it, got excited and suggested that while the nurses went to lunch they play *manille* with some North

African *bicots* in the room used for bandaging. That was forbidden. Again Cascade won everything. It was phenomenal luck. A noncom from the Salle Saint-Grévin next to us who was passing by couldn't get over it. He took Cascade to the place where the noncoms were, to play poker with them. Cascade won again and again. Finally he got up all pale and stopped playing entirely.

"It's not good," Cascade said.

"It couldn't be better," I said. "It's amazing."

That was an attempt to cheer him up. He did not share my opinion. We went back to our beds for the doctor's rounds. Méconille came by with two broads from outside and a guy in mufti we'd never seen before. When he stopped in front of Cascade's bed Cascade said:

"I'd like you to cut off my foot, Doctor. It's not good for walking anymore ..."

Méconille looked very upset, though he usually never turned down any chance to amputate.

"We'll have to wait a little longer, my boy ... It's too early ..."

But it was obvious that Méconille was holding something back. He wouldn't have spoken like that normally. The other little shits didn't think it was natural of him either. It was extremely weird.

Cascade had made the attempt. He fell back into the cot.

"Should we go out?" he asked.

We gobbled down a huge helping in the kitchen, some rice, and then we went out.

I thought we'd go to the Hyperbole but he didn't want to.

"We'll go to the side that looks out to the country."

He walked quickly all the same despite his foot. Still we couldn't get nabbed by the gendarmes. They were getting worse and worse. If you didn't have regular permission it was a real drama every time — L'Espinasse had had to go herself to get us out of the gendarmerie. The English cops weren't any better, and the Belgians were even filthier. We walked as if we were on a battlefield from one landmark to the next and finally we reached the side by the country as he called it, a place behind the town and away from the front. Peace. You could hardly hear the cannon from there. We sat down on an embankment. We looked. Far, far away there was still sun and trees, soon it would be full summer. But the patches of passing clouds stayed a long time on the beet fields. I do think that's pretty. But the northern suns are fragile. On our left the sleepy canal flowed by under the wind-filled poplars. It zigzagged, murmuring things up to the hills and kept flowing all the way to the sky which continued it in blue before the tallest of the three smokestacks on the tip of the horizon.

I wanted to talk but I held myself back. After what happened yesterday, I wanted him to be the one to start. The thing with the cards also demanded an explanation. I don't think he cheated. It was luck.

In an enclosure we saw some workers and all the monks, old ones, working, but they were taking it easy. They were pruning espaliers. It was the monastery garden. Farther on, here and there in the furrows, a farmer was turning over dirt with his ass in the air. He was digging up beets.

"Beets are huge around Peurdu-sur-la-Lys," I remarked.

"Come on," Cascade said. "Should we go see where it goes?"

"How far?" I said very surprised.

It didn't seem very sensible in our state to go strolling about for pleasure.

"I'm not going far," I said.

We set off straight ahead, though. We turned our backs to the town.

"We're getting too far away," I said. "We'll never have time to get back."

He didn't answer. I told myself it wasn't worth being hauled back in as a deserter now that I had the medal.

"I'll go another half mile," I said, "and then I'm going back."

It's true that I also threw up twice on the way.

"You puke all the time," he actually said.

It was mean to say that to me. Fine. We didn't go even a thousand more yards. Barely three hundred yards on, a clown popped out from behind a sentry box, with his bayonet fixed to his musket—a real fury.

After he'd shouted a good long time he asked us where we were going.

"We're just taking a walk in the country."

We didn't back down. Then he put his weapon down and explained that they were waiting for a whole army of reinforcements on this road and also that the Germans were just at hill-level now, at the end of the fields, in the place where the little canal went. That in scarcely three or four hours we'd be bombed too if we stayed there. That we had to clear off fast.

No sooner said than done, hobbling as we were. It was blocked everywhere. We fell back to the canal after these explanations. We had to go around in absurd circles Cascade and me, with his idiotic whims. We get back to the canal bank. I see my friend frown deeply and he sets off toward the water.

"You make me laugh," I say, to try to cut through the sort of murk he'd been stuck in since that infamous lunch with Monsieur Harnache the day before. "You make me laugh, you don't know anything at all for certain, you don't even know if Angèle really did what she says, but you're scared stiff ... She's so stuck up I'm sure she said everything in front of everyone just to humiliate you ... and that she has the letter in her pocket ..."

The corner of his mouth turned up when he heard me, on purpose, scornfully.

"With you, you can really say you're sick—so you don't even see how it's all connected…"

I didn't understand. So I shut up. I had my opinion, that's all. I still had some money, 25 francs from my parents and he must have had as much too from Angèle.

"I'll go get some wine," I say.

"Bring back three liters, that'll do you good."

He tells me that.

The café was near the town, at the entrance to the canal. I'd need about a quarter of an hour round trip.

"You're not coming with me?" I say.

"I don't want to," he says. "I'm going to go see if I can find a pole at the lock to fish."

I set calmly off, wrapped up in my thoughts. Behind me I hear a big *splash!* in the water. Even before I turned around I knew. I turn around. Over there, at the lock, the load that had splattered was of course Cascade. It was just us on the canal.

"Are you drowning?" I shout.

I don't know why. It was intuition too. His head was above the water at the same level as both his hands. He wasn't drowning at all. He was extricating himself from the mud. I go back. I scream my head off at him.

"It's too shallow," I say to him, "you sucker! It's too shallow. You're just shit-deep—it's hilarious!"

He cut up nasty then did Cascade. Fortunately there was no one there to see us when he was being an asshole.

"You can't drown yourself there you idiot, it isn't deep enough. I would've told you…"

He hoists himself up onto the grassy bank, with difficulty because of his foot.

"You're not drowned but you'll get the shivers and a shitty cold," I say.

He didn't rise to the bait.

"Go find some rum and leave me alone," he replies.

That's how he answers me. I go back again. This time I bring back a whole quart of rum, a quart of beer and two of white wine and three brioches bigger than our heads. We lean against a poplar. We guzzle it down in a big way. We felt well fed. We knocked it back.

"I want to catch some fish."

"I dunno how," I say.

"I'll show you."

It's fine, suddenly I was dead drunk. I follow the canal bank to the café to rent the poles. They give me some along with some maggots, a little box full. We toast each other again and get to it. We cast, the corks plop in.

Scarcely had he dipped in his hook than he caught a real pike, and then some small fry, enough to fill a basket. I catch nothing, naturally. He has all the luck. By five o'clock there's nothing left in the bottles. At six o'clock the daylight fades.

"Gotta bring back the fish," he says.

So we start on our way. We get back without any difficulty to the Virginal Secours.

"It's the Miraculous Catch of the Fish!" the nun said, the one who cooked and also carried the mail.

We didn't get the reference. Still you don't stay drunk for long in such conditions. After vomiting just once or twice, I was already completely sober. We were too worried, so to speak. We had the night in front of us. And a night that was looking to be very thick and very treacherous. Soup first as usual. But then Cascade didn't want to go to bed. He went from the toilet to the window in the hallway. L'Espinasse was making her rounds, and the concierge was dimming the gas when she passed behind Cascade without seeming to see him and then, pausing in front of me, she stood there for a minute.

"Is it you," I said. "Is it you?"

She didn't answer. She stayed there another minute maybe and then she sort of slipped away into the half-light.

Then the night really started.

Cascade sat down on the bed instead of getting into it. He started reading, even though he almost never read. He read by candlelight. His neighbor wasn't happy about it, the one opposite wasn't either, especially since there were two guys who kept groaning and another one who wanted to piss all the time. The night nurse came to blow out his candle. He relit it. It was already eleven o'clock. He had read all the papers. He looked for something to read from the center table. He lit the candle again. Then the artilleryman from Morocco with cystitis, the one by the door, the one who snored the loudest of all of us, a real thug, threw his cane across the room at the candle. Cascade gets up and wants to bash his face in. It almost turned into a disaster. They called each other assholes at the top of their voices.

"Fine," said Cascade, "if it's like that I'll go read in the toilet, at least I won't see your filthy faces anymore, since I'm keeping you from jerking off in peace, you fucking fags."

That did it. At the other end, the old Army guy from the 12th, a real veteran who was full of diabetes, gets up. He flings his piss-pot with all his might across the line of twenty-two cots and sprinkles the whole bunch. It smashes into a window. Two nuns appear, everyone's quiet. And then it starts up again. Finally Cascade who's still there says:

"I don't want to sleep anymore. You can all fuck off."

He wants to light the candle again.

"Go screw yourself, you dirty asshole!"

"Let them shoot that guy for real!"

"Tell him to fuck off and leave us alone!"

That shows they'd had enough.

So that's what happens. Cascade goes to the toilet to sit down since it's the place where the gas was lit all night.

It must have been one in the morning.

"Hey Ferdinand, do you have anything else to read?"

I looked in the nurses' room. I knew where they hid their books, a hat box. *Les Belles Images** — there were entire volumes. Cascade took everything. He was enthralled believe me.

"Close the door," I said, "if someone comes . . ."

He closed the door. One hour and then two went by. He was still locked in, I didn't dare get up so the others wouldn't shout again.

Finally the faintest daylight crept over the opposite roof . . . the one with all the lacy edging.

And then a voice that made everyone jump, a very soft voice though, a funny voice for a gendarme, almost a woman's voice, but very precise, a voice that knew what it wanted, at the entrance to the hall leading to the Salle Saint-Gonzef:

"You do have here the soldier Gontran Cascade, from the 392nd infantry regiment, don't you?"

"He's in the toilet next to you, gendarme," the other artilleryman, the one near the door, said at the top of his voice.

The door opened.

Cascade came out. *Click, click* we heard the handcuffs.

There was another cop waiting at the end of the hallway. There was no time to see Cascade again, his face I mean. It was still too dark.

Four days later he was executed near Péronne at the billet where his regiment the 418th infantry were taking two weeks' leave.

* *Les Belles Images* was a children's weekly created in 1904.

They pissed me off, the guys in the ward with their feats of arms. When we learned that Cascade had in the end been executed, they all started talking bullshit about their exploits. Suddenly they were all heroes. It was as if they were making excuses for having been so shitty to him during those last hours. They'd sullied him. They didn't talk about him but it bothered them, I could see. Listening to them, you'd think nothing in the war scared them. The veteran guy Giboune, the one who was still shitting in his pants when the noon plane passed over the ward, he never stopped crowing about his little wound. It had taken at least three machine guns to make that flesh wound in his ass. Like that. Ablukum, the Moroccan Goumier with the boils, who thought of nothing but his fistula, had never actually seen any bullets but that didn't prevent him from storming, so he said, a whole native camp in Morocco all by himself with a torch and a shout—all on his own. He'd terrified them he claimed. It's because of Cascade they were talking such crap. I think secretly they were all pretty depressed. They were filling themselves up with lies to resist the twists of fate. I was better filled up than they were because of my medal and my cushy citation, but I still wasn't confident. Because of my experiences I was aging a month a week. That's the speed you have to go at in order not to be shot in the war. Believe me.

In any case they were jealous. I didn't flash my medal though. I only put it on when I went out to town. Now that Cascade had gone I had no one to support me if I staggered in a dizzy spell. I didn't fraternize much with the other guys. In the ward we were all starting to be parasites. Heroic as we were more or less, we were all absolute hypocrites. The proof is that we never talked about L'Espinasse or about what happened below in the lazaretto. We only let slip what we wanted to. The most seriously wounded, the ones who dribbled the most, kept all their real intentions to themselves. The dying ones weren't sincere. I saw some, when L'Espinasse was going by, pretend to be dying. It's a fact. I observed her carefully the bitch with her heavenly veils as she petted the most damaged ones, as she was preparing her very pleasurable probings, and I said to myself that in the end she might have been right. She was looking for sincerity, the others didn't have any. She gave me courage, L'Espinasse, with her manner. When she stopped by at night to kiss me, I stuck my tongue hard into her gums. I hurt her a little then. I knew it was sensitive. I was beginning to understand her, I'm a sincere guy. Which means she was becoming attached. One time she whispers to me:

"Ferdinand I've come to an agreement with headquarters. Because of your ear trouble, while you wait for your appearance before the board, you can sleep in the little pavilion at the end of our garden. We made up a bed for you and you'll be more relaxed there. No one will bother you …"

That was something to hear. I was beginning to know the girl, and all her wicked ways. It was a funny way to isolate me in her pavilion. In the end I move. I give my spot to someone else.

"You won't ever see me again, you fuckers. You're all going back to the front. I'm the one who'll be snacking on you when you've all turned into vegetables below between the beets and the sewage."

They had a good laugh. They weren't mean about the joke.

"Asshole, count your filthy guts, fucking idiot, you can go fuck your medal …"

It was tit for tat.

I move in. I inspect the pavilion. It was OK. It seemed like a decent place, at the end of the garden. Very isolated. Nothing to complain about. They brought me my mess tin. I could go out she said, from ten to five.

I go along the little streets. I vomit discreetly under the porches when I have to. Apparently the front is thirty miles away everywhere now, in front and behind. I think about where I'd go if I split. The earth is rotten everywhere, I said to myself. I'd have to go to a foreign country where they're not killing each other. But I had no health, no money, nothing. It's sickening when for months you've seen convoys of men in all sorts of uniforms marching in the streets like rows of sausages, soldiers, reserves, in sky-blue, apple-green, supported by wheels pushing the whole mess of mincemeat to the big grinder for fools. They march straight ahead, hum songs, down a drink, come back horizontal, bleed, down another drink, weep, shout, they're rotting away already then, a shower of rain, now the wheat is growing, other fools arrive by boat, it bellows, it's in a hurry to unload everything, on the water the big blower spins round, turns asswise, the lovely ship at the jetty, now it's off again, carving the foaming waves looking for others ... Always happy, the idiots, always partying. The more they are crushed to pieces, the better the flowers grow, that's my opinion. Long live shit and good wine. All for nothing!

What did I risk by going back to the Hyperbole? Nothing. I'd give the girl Destinée the news, if she didn't know yet. But Angèle had already filled her in. She never left town Angèle. Of course not. She had contacts here. I understood that too. The Place Majeure was getting more and more crowded, like a crossroads of all worlds. People were piled on top of each other. They'd put down planks so the streets that intersected could be more easily walked over. There were more dead every day because of the bombings and the crowds of troopers, but we'd never overflowed into the surrounding area so much. At the market it was monstrous. Flowers especially, people tore them away. It's extraordinary how bouquets make the war go by. For many reasons. They had a siren, in case of danger from the air, and everyone supposedly took cover in basements. It was magnificent to see. I saw a whole battalion stay at the Hyperbole for an hour while the alarm sounded. Nothing was left when it left, not one glass. They'd drunk the crystal. I'm not making it up. A 75 cannon was posted with its horses at the notary's on the second floor, he was so afraid. There you go—that shows you how all hell was breaking loose.

When it was calm, Angèle came out into the street, the widow. At first I didn't dare approach her, she was standing not far from the English headquarters as before. Just diagonally across from where, behind the half curtain at the Hyperbole, I was watching her. Destinée hadn't understood much at first, the huge misfortune that had befallen Cascade. Her nature wasn't one that understood. She cried sincerely when she thought of him but she didn't really know why. She went on staying in the same room above the café with Angèle since it had been arranged like that. And also she was very tired, Destinée was, because she served all the different kinds of alcohol and aperitifs from casks, all by herself, for the thirty-five tables at the Hyperbole, from 6:15 AM until ten at night, which were the opening hours set by the regulations. And then there was Angèle whose wickedness was unbelievable: I found out later that she found a way to go down on Destinée when she came back with her and make her come two, three times. And the more tired Destinée was from serving, the more excited Angèle was to make her come, and the harder it was, the better it seemed to her. People are rabid.

In short it wasn't a very decent time to go see Angèle after what had happened, but she saw me coming without surprise. We went to another café to talk. I didn't dare reproach her. She tempted me though. I'd have liked for her to explain. She avoided that part of the conversation. I dropped Cascade to get closer to her and feel her up a little. She let me. It was hard for me because of my arm which almost made me scream when I squeezed hard and my ear which was so full of noise that it would explode when my face became flushed. I still got a hard-on, that was the main thing. I put aside all my bleeding parts and imagined her ass tense with expectation. I was seeing life again. Good Angèle. She could sense I was all tumescent. She had very dark velvety eyes, full of sweetness like Cascade's song, the one he'd never sing again. She captured my whole heart. She's the one who paid for all the drinks. I didn't want to ask my parents for money anymore. I was proud and disgusted.

"You're right," she encouraged me.

I watched her walk away through the Place Majeure. She passed between the resting battalions like the very spirit of joy and happiness. Her buttocks carved a graceful furrow through the middle of a hundred stinking tons of exhaustion sprawling there in twenty thousand men, dying of thirst. The square smelled so strongly that she hurried through it at those times. And then she turned round to powder her face, that was her favorite thing to do, at a nice distance from the headquarters of General V. W. Purcell. He went out at eleven o'clock with his two chestnut horses did General V. W. Purcell, in his yellow and purple cabriolet, to make a little tour of the trenches. He drove himself without ostentation. He was a man of the world. A good ways behind, two mounted officers followed him — the Irish major B.K.K. Olisticle and Lt. Percy O'Hairie, a real lady with his elegance and svelteness.

Angèle's thing was to pick up English officers, nothing but Brits, upper class ones, the kind that are afraid of being seen fucking. One day, two days, I understood. I didn't dare ask to go to her bedroom. It was delicate. She's the one who offered.

"Listen," she said, "with your medal you're nice, you're a good sort. You wouldn't know what I had in my head last night as I slept with Destinée ... No? ... Well I was saying to myself that you'd be good at making a scandal, you would ... you could be my husband ... I did it in Paris with 'Dédé little hands,' it always works and it's easy too."

I let her explain.

"So, I get undressed, right, as usual, I let the guy rub himself a little ... When he's hard, very hard, I suck him ... Then you come into the room all of a sudden without knocking. I didn't lock it on purpose to pretend. I say Shit! It's my husband ... You can imagine the look the English get then ... There was one I did at the Olympia, he got sick ... They're the ones who offer cash, it's always them, you don't need to worry, they know ... I've done the trick twenty times with Dédé and I tell you it's ready money ... There's nothing more idiotic than the English when they have a hard-on and [a few illegible words] blokes ... They're all idiots when they see you come in. They don't know how to excuse themselves for having it out in the open. It's so funny. Then I act the one who's been compromised. I cry out, I'm secretly laughing my head off. It's a real acting display. You'll see. If you don't want to, just say ... You won't regret it, but I'm the one who decides how much you get ..."

"OK!" I said.

I was all for women's emancipation. I was sick of being broke, of being in pieces from my head and ideas and ear to my asshole, I wanted to mend myself in one way or another.

"I'll take care of you. I'll let you fuck like you've never ... If you're nice, if you're a good boy, you can eat out my ass the way I like ... It will be as if we're married. First though, I'm two years older than you, I'm the one in charge ..."

It was intriguing, her choice of words, and as I listened she made my imagination leap with joy. I couldn't restrain myself. So long as there's vice there's pleasure. Still I had a little thought for the Cascade boy but then I came back to myself and the little thought wasn't there anymore. The whole present was all for Angèle, everything for sex. That's where salvation lay. First of all, this wasn't the moment to dissolve into scruples. It was the time for giving up all those things drummed in by education. The blow that had stunned me so deeply had somehow rid me of an enormous weight of conscience, the weight of education as they call it—I'd won that at least. Ah! Even if you looked closely, I didn't have it anymore. I was sick and tired of going from day to day without using my skull, especially from one night to the next with my parachuting sensations and my foundry head. I owed nothing to humanity anymore, at least not to the humanity you believe in when you're twenty with scruples fat as cockroaches scuttling between all minds and things. Angèle came just in time to replace my father and even Cascade who still had something prewar about him, or so I thought. Angèle was a pleasure lover, she had a taste for the foreign, for trade.

Fine. If I was going to replace Cascade I had to show I was up to snuff from the beginning, that's to say much more liberated. I reflect and then I commit myself.

"OK," I say, "count me in for everything."

She takes me to her digs, Destinée's that is, to explain what I should do, she directs me in short. I had to knock on the door that was to the left of the bed, in the middle between the toilet and the trunk. It was actually a closet, it stank of sweat. As a room it was pretty shabby, but that excited them more, she said.

"Because you know, those people already have too much luxury at home ..."

As guarantee, she gets undressed. It's the first time I saw her in a slip. She was the undulating kind naked and not very tall, pretty tiny even, delicate in short but tough. Right away I see what's happening with her. Along with the eyes it's the skin. There's no mirage like it, it looks like no other. You can manage to defend yourself with different girls, you have some way to resist if necessary the waves on the skin of blondes, the silkiness of brunettes, the fleshy ones that is, the successful ones, they're tempting to touch like life itself, with all your fingers, it resists a little, it lingers, it's the fruit of paradise, that goes without saying. It has no limits, but still you've developed little ways of resisting ... Whereas the redhead brings out the animal right away. It comes out, asking nothing, it has recognized its sister, it is happy.

So here I am eating out Angèle right in the middle of the mattress. It made me buzzed too, with throbbing pulsations. I thought I'd die from it. She still came for me, once, twice without stopping. It was nothing for her. I bit the inside of her thighs. Punishing her a little. Then she really starts enjoying herself. But I couldn't go on. I get up to vomit a little—I pretend just to spit.

I had to learn the trick with the closet. It was late. You can still see the Place Majeure in the distance which didn't stop living its own life of the flesh, circulating between the sirens. There was a light on in the English headquarters. Though that was forbidden.

"Tomorrow don't forget to be here at one. You'll wait in here till I bring a man back. They can't see us together in the street. When you hear footsteps in the stairway, you'll hide and look through the keyhole. When I'm naked and he's in position you smack him a good one and look surprised ... The rest, you'll see, that'll happen all by itself."

I'm in a hurry to get back to my pavilion. It was a little unsettling my way of being isolated at the end of the garden. I couldn't make any plans there were so many things still to be afraid of. L'Espinasse came to do my bandages and put drops in my ear. There was wind and rain from a storm outside and the dogs barking when she left. You have to imagine situations like that.

I held on to myself to go to sleep. I always had to make a huge effort not to give in to the anxiety of not being able to sleep anymore, nevermore because of the buzzing that will never stop, it will never stop until life stops. I'm sorry. I go on about it but that's how the song goes. Oh well, let's not be sad. The next day, as I was saying, there I was, inside that is, between the trunk and the toilet. I didn't wait long, an hour maybe, a soft well-modulated voice as they say. I peer out. It's a Scot, he takes off his little skirt, he's naked very quickly. He's a redhead too and pretty muscular, like a horse. He starts slowly, he doesn't speak. He looks like a chestnut stallion on top of her. It's very simple. Walk, trot, gallop, and then he leaps over the fence, one stroke, another, not violent, he fills her up, how beautiful it is. She grimaces he plows her so deep. I said she was fragile. She looks over to where I am. Hey hey, she mouths.

She grimaces even more. She can't keep from coming, him too. He squeezes her ass so much it looks like she'll lift up his belly he's squeezing her so hard.

His hands fascinate me while he works away, they're crampons on Angèle's skin, splayed crampons, muscled and hairy like the rest of him. I should have emerged from the closet, played the indignant husband at that point, that was my chance. Especially since after he came he waited a good while, still without speaking, his penis exposed, he just panted a little like someone who had been running too much. I wonder how he'd have reacted?

Then, just barely after he got his wind back, he mounted her again. She was still panting. He started everything all over again.

She barely reacted anymore the Scot was so powerful. Even inside my compartment you could still hear the cannon in the distance, on both sides of the town now. I had a hard-on. I was buzzing. I was almost suffocating in my cell, especially since I had to crouch down to see them. I wondered if he was going to kill the kid finally, he was giving her such a pounding between her thighs, the stud. Not at all. She let herself be carried like a package in the end. She was more than supple. Only she groaned a little! He had put her on his stomach, him on his back that is. She was pale. I was so gripped by the spectacle and was clinging so close to the door that it suddenly burst open onto their fury, there, just below them. I say to myself this isn't going to end well. The beefy guy is definitely going to lay me out ... Not at all. He doesn't even pause. He goes on plowing her. Even harder maybe since I'm watching him. It disconcerts me I confess. The kid was almost unconscious on the guy who was completely naked and very hairy. She'd stopped reacting. She let herself be flipped over in a roar. There's a man who hadn't fucked in months. *Hup!* He fucked her some more at a gallop. She was trying to get him off her to cry out. He was stifling her with his mouth. Finally he came with another massive stroke brutal to the point of tears stretching his legs straight out as if he'd had something shoved right up his asshole.

I thought he'd kill her then he came so much. On each side of his buttocks there were huge furrows he was so squeezed into the kid. And then very slowly he relaxed as if he too were dead and he stayed there very gently, for at least three minutes on her. I didn't move. He grunted and then he looked over at me and smiled very kindly at me. Not annoyed at all. He puts one foot on the floor, then stands up and gets dressed next to the window and he still doesn't say anything to me. He searches through his pocket, gets out a pound, puts it in the kid's hand who was still lying there, stunned, getting her breath back.

Feeling the pound she recovers her breath and looks at us both. That surprised her. The Scot was dressed with his skirt, his baldric and his little dagger, very content. He leans down to kiss her, kisses her still saying nothing and leaves. He closes the door very quietly. There's a guy who wasn't easily ruffled. Angèle had trouble standing up. She felt below her belly with both her hands. She moved carefully forward to wash her vulva in the bidet. She was still panting, me too.

"That was like a storm," I say, always the poet.

"Maybe," she replies, "and you're nothing, you asshole."

There was no answer to that.

"Tomorrow," she says, "you won't wait in the closet. You'll stay on the corner opposite, on the terrace of the Hyperbole, and then you'll watch the window carefully when I close the curtain, see? And then you'll come up ... You won't knock on the door. You'll open it. You understand?"

"Yes," I say.

"Then beat it."

I want to kiss her.

"Here eat his cum."

And she held out a handful of it ... I didn't insist on the kiss, I didn't want to annoy her, I didn't have the wherewithal.

I didn't have a good night either. I wondered if I failed again to help her swindle her client how Angèle would react. Angèle was my only hope.

In Peurdu-sur-la-Lys, they had to evacuate all the sick and wounded, especially the ones who could already walk. The town wasn't safe anymore at all. On the Place Majeure there was constant vertigo because of the explosions. The water trough was destroyed. The town was so easily sighted that the regiments passing through took cover as quickly as they could, they rushed into the little streets as if there were a fire. The panic was sometimes worse than in battles and there were fits of laughter too because of the cafés that stayed open till the last minute. I saw one guy, a Zouave, come right up to the bar at the Hyperbole, pushed by a bunch of soldiers that a shell had thrown together under the arcades. The guy just has time to order a kir! He crumples in half. He was done in. We were all stunned there between the tables. Had to drink fast. You get the idea.

The next day at one, early, I take my position where Angèle had told me to. I wait for things. Luck would have it that it was almost calm. Free from the endless train of equipment, the thirst and dust of the convoys constantly passing through, the racket of little trucks pushing all the armies, to the end of wars, from one trembling wheel to the other, with the sagging chain, with two old nags always stumbling together, with 2,300 axles screaming for oil, echoing like hail hitting and filling the whole street until it's gone by. [Illegible sentence.] An hour passes. I say to myself Angèle can't find a trick. The siesta hour when Englishmen like to fuck has passed, at night they're too drunk. But a lot of people were coming out of the English headquarters, well-fed ones. Fat ones, old ones, young ones, all kinds, on horse, on foot, even in automobiles. Maybe I've been ditched? I said to myself simply.

Another hour watching things. Destinée comes over to me. She hadn't understood anything either. I don't explain. She makes friendly advances. It's fine.

Good. The curtain moves, I'm not mistaken, on the second floor. I hurry as fast as I can. I'm definitely resolved. I even forbid myself to have dizzy spells. One floor. Two floors. I don't knock on the door. I stumble in. The guy in the sack on top of Angèle leaps up. It was an old guy, he was just wearing khaki boxers. He was bare-chested. There's a look of terror on his face. Mine too. We're both terrified. Suddenly Angèle bursts out laughing.

"That's my husband!" she said laughing her head off. "That's my husband!"

He quickly stuffs his prick back into his fly. He's trembling all over, me too. He's too scared to see we were pretending. He's afraid, which bucks me up.

"Money! Money!" I say then in English. "Money!" all the while trembling and courageous with [illegible word].

Angèle insisted in English:

"My husband! Yes! *Mon mari!* My husband! My husband!"

She was all sprawled on the bed, making crazy gestures. She kept repeating the word "husband" which she'd remembered right away.

"This one's a pushover Ferdinand. Hit him in the face," she urges me in good French.

It's true that he was a gift for a beginner like me. No two days are the same. I work up my nerve, use my left not too hard. I flatten his cheek a little. Deep down I'm afraid of hurting him.

"Hit him hard, idiot," she says.

I start again. It was easy, he wasn't defending himself. He had white hair, he was at least fifty. I hit him hard right on the nose. It bleeds. Then Angèle changes her tune. She starts crying. She flings herself on his neck.

"Protect me, protect me," she whispers to him. "Take me now. Fuck me now," she says softly to me, "fathead. Fuck me."

I hesitate.

"Do what I tell you asshole. Get out your prick."

I take it out. But she's still holding the guy by the neck. She clasps him and I clasp her. She stands still so I can screw her. She cries on his face. She comes like a fountain. He turned every color you can imagine, I must say. He was holding his nose. She was rummaging in his fly. We were all panting.

"Slap me now," she orders me.

That at least I did wholeheartedly. I give her a good dozen, enough to set off a donkey. Then he thinks the beating is going to start over again.

"No!" he shouts. "No!"

He leaps over to the pocket of his tunic on the chair. He shows me his cash, a fistful of greenbacks.

"Don't take them," she says to me. "Get dressed and scram."

I button myself up and tidy up. He kept insisting, he absolutely wanted me to take the money. I didn't hear what he said. I was buzzing too much. I go over to the bucket they used as a toilet to vomit. He helps me compassionately, he holds my head, no anger.

Angèle spoke English. She explained to him:

"*My husband. His honor,* it's made him sick! Sick! Sick!"

I was laughing my head off while I was throwing up. He was hairy the john, up to the shoulders. His chest hair all gray actually. He didn't know where to look.

"Forgive me! Forgive me!" he said to me.

I left without acknowledging him, proudly so to say. I waited in the stairway for half an hour. And then I went back to my digs, I couldn't wait any more. I couldn't stand up. I hope it works, I said to myself.

After lunch Angèle comes in person, smiling. That reassured me.

"How much did he give you?"

"That's none of your business," she says, "but everything's fine."

She was pale though, I notice.

"First of all he's not what you'd expect, that English guy, he's worth more than that!"

"Oh!" I say. "How did you find that out?"

"We talked, that's all."

She told me I didn't understand the finer points.

"So? What did you decide?"

"Well listen! When you left I told him you were a mean one! That you were making a martyr of me! That you were jealous and as depraved as anything! …The more I told him the more he wanted me to say … So I wanted to see if he was really rich. It's not easy to be sure. They always lie where cash is concerned … But I wanted to find out before saving myself for that idiot, because can you believe it—he immediately offered to take me to England …"

"Really?!"

"And then he wants to get me a job there. How old do you think he is …?"

"About fifty."

"Fifty-two, he showed me his papers, everything. I had him show me everything. He's an engineer… In engineering… He's an engineer, actually he's better than that, he owns three factories in London, that's what."

I saw she was very happy, but I could see she was already elsewhere.

"So what about me?"

"He's not angry at you, silly! I made him understand that you were really a good guy except for your big flaws and your violence, which you'd learned in the war, that you had to be forgiven because you were badly wounded in the ear and in the head and you were even the bravest guy in your regiment, your medal proves it. He wants to see you again … He wants to do something for you too—"

"Shit."

I didn't understand.

"Tomorrow at three o'clock we'll all meet at the café where the canal ends, you know, at the lock. Go on then, go have a nice little jerk-off, I'll see you later, I don't want to keep Destinée waiting, she's afraid of the dark, she locks the door downstairs."

So she clears off.

Fifteen more hours on the clock to get through, I say to myself, before the meeting. I don't want to go out. I could feel all around me a fate that was so fragile it was like the creaking floorboards all round, and in the furniture whenever I walked around in the digs. Finally I stopped moving. I waited. Around midnight some fabric in the hallway moves, it was L'Espinasse.

"Are you OK, Ferdinand?" she asks me from behind the door.

Am I going to answer you, I ask myself. Am I going to answer you? In a tiny voice that sounds almost asleep I say:

"I'm fine Madame, I'm fine ..."

"Goodnight then Ferdinand, goodnight."

She didn't come back.

The next day at the canal, I go past the little terrace by the dive. I pass the lock and stand waiting behind the poplar there, a good hundred and fifty feet away, invisible. I watch. I don't want to make myself stand out. Just look first. I wait. I was beginning to learn how to use nature, it's all just a matter of waiting. She arrives first and sits down. She orders a shandy. It's funny the fashions in '14, they didn't last long. It's already the complete opposite in '15. A felt cloche that looks like a helmet, which she pulled down over her eyes with a little veil and which made her eyes look even larger since that was the only thing in her face. Those eyes bothered me even from as far away as I was. There's no doubt she had influence, Angèle, over the mysterious regions of the soul as they say.

The other idiot arrived, the "engineer" Englishman, very slowly by the towpath. He had a little bit of a paunch. Dressed, it's funny, he wore his fifty years more than he did naked.

His uniform was khaki like all the others and he must have been from headquarters because he wore the red band on his cap, and the stick of course and the boots which were worth a good 500 francs.

He sits opposite Angèle's eyes and then they talk. When they've talked for a good while I approach limping to seem badly wounded. I look at him dispassionately and he looks very decent and even quite kind. I sit down. I make myself comfortable. He looks at me tenderly, that's the truth. Angèle too. Little by little I start to feel like their child. We order four beers, and a full meal for me. They both spoil me. Then I think it was just across the way that I saw Cascade try to drown himself—I bring this memory up from my mud. I hide it. I say nothing. Angèle is very forgetful in any case. The major asks my name. I give it. He gives me his. Cecil B. Purcell his name is, Major Cecil B. Purcell K.B.B. He hands me his card, it's printed there. He's from the Corps of Engineers, it's printed on another piece of paper. His wallet is full, stuffed with cash actually. I ogle it. With what I see there's enough to go round the world twelve times, so many times you can't be found anymore.

"Listen Ferdinand. He wants to take both of us to England, the nice uncle."

That's how she'd been calling him since yesterday, the uncle.

As he goes on looking at me his eyes get wet. He likes me. She watches him liking me. We've caught a good one, make no mistake.

The pretty sun of great occasions shines on both sides of the canal. Summer is celebrating us, welcoming us with its ardors.

Another beer. Everyone wants to do me good. We were all stammering in the heat, patting each other on the shoulders and it's the affection of a fine friendship. It's become easy and natural for me to slur my words, now that I seem very drunk. I just have to let myself be carried away by my phenomena and my little personal memories, it happens all by itself. In the blink of an eye, I'm transposed into the surreal with my torrent of music on tap.

He runs his hand through my hair, K.B.B. Purcell. He's having a good time too. Everything's going well. Angèle was holding her own all the same.

"Get a move on Ferdinand," she whispers as we were getting up, "we're clearing off in two days. Tell your shitty bitch that you want to convalesce in London, that he's a relative and he'll take care of you."

That's what we agree.

It's true that I had a good grounding. England didn't exactly remind me of favorable circumstances, but it was still better than what they'd made me endure since then.

"OK!" I say.

I feel happy too, I'm the one leading them both. We wander over to the towpath arm in arm, supporting each other. We don't go far. Purcell between us. We sit down on the grassy embankment. From here we have a clear view of the lock where Cascade ... That is ... His song comes to my mouth:

I know it well ...
That you are pretty ...
That your big eyes full of sweetness ...

He liked hearing me sing, Purcell did. He liked everything about me. It broke my heart. I couldn't give him more than two verses. He wanted to learn everything, Purcell, he wanted me to write it down for him.

The fucking cannon never stopped. When it wasn't there I produced them on my own. Even today I can reproduce perfectly imitated cannon booms. Finally the evening came to an end.

"Kiss her," I said to Purcell, "kiss her," when we separated.

And I can't say that that wasn't sincere. There are feelings we're wrong not to encourage, they'd restore the world I say.

We're the victims of prejudices. We don't dare, we don't dare say Kiss her! It says everything though, it says the happiness of the world. That was Purcell's opinion too. We parted friends then. He was my future, Purcell, my new life. I explained everything when I went back to L'Espinasse. I went to find her at the Virginal Secours on purpose for that. She looked glum. Then I spoke differently … In the little room I stood up for myself then, for the first time in my fucking existence, probably. There weren't three hours to lose.

"I have to go," I said. "I have to go or I'll go to headquarters and tell them you feed on dead guys."

I had no witnesses. It was brazen. She could have had me court-martialed for slander. There wasn't a single guy in the Salle Saint-Gonzef who would have stood witness for me. They hadn't seen anything. They didn't know anything, that's for sure. Plus they detested me with my idiotic medal and my extra freedoms.

"If you don't let me have six months' leave, you understand, six whole months of leave, I don't have anything left to lose … as sure as my name is Ferdinand, I'll find you wherever you are and I'll stick my saber in your belly so you'll have trouble getting up. You understand?"

I would have done it too. I had my future to defend.

"For England!" I added. "For England."

"Are you really considering it Ferdinand?"

"I'm considering it. I'm considering it. I'm considering nothing but that."

"What will you do over there Ferdinand?"

"Look after your own ass," I replied like Cascade.

Those were funny ways to talk, but still it worked.

Two days later I left for Boulogne, with a nice travel pass. I was wary at the station. I was wary boarding the ship. It was all too beautiful. Even the torturing sounds became exciting. Never had I heard anything so magnificent as the ship's horn piercing the racket in my ear. The ship was there at the wharf for me. It was panting, the monster. Purcell and the kid must already have been in London since that morning. There was no war in London. Even the cannon you couldn't hear anymore. Scarcely, that is one or two *booms* from time to time very rarely, very soft, over there, farther than the last wave of the sea line on the horizon, farther than the sky you could say.

There were a lot of civilians on the boat—they were reassuring, they spoke like before we were condemned to death, about this and that. They arranged their little things very comfortably for the crossing. It's strange and touching to see the boat, the horn too, the good, the beautiful, the huge boat. It shook all its carcass, it shuddered rather. The surface of the dock shuddered suddenly for real. We slid alongside the black docks from the jetties to [illegible word]. The waves came. *Hup!* They crashed onto us. *Hup* ... bigger! We fell back down. It was raining.

Seventy francs I had to travel with, I remember. Agathe had sewn them into my pocket before leaving. Good Agathe. We'd see each other again.

The two jetties became tiny above the surging foam, snug around their little lighthouse. The town shrank behind them. It melted into the sea too. And everything toppled over into the scenery of clouds, into the huge shoulder of the open sea. All the rubbish was over, it had spread all its manure over the earth of France, buried its millions of suppurating killers, its copses, its corpses, its multicrap towns and its infinite sons of myriadshit guys. There was nothing more, the sea had taken everything, covered everything. Long live the sea! Now I just had to worry about vomiting. I couldn't take it anymore. I had all the vertigos of a boat in my own insides. The war had given me too a sea, for me alone, a rumbling one, a noise-filled one in my own head. Long live war! There was no more coast now, a thin edge maybe, very thin, close by at the end of the wind. To the left of the dock over there was still Flanders, then you couldn't see it anymore.

I never saw Destinée again in fact. I never even heard any news of her. The owners of the Hyperbole must have made a fortune so they fired her. It's funny there are beings who seem loaded with baggage, they come from infinity, set down before you their heavy baggage of emotions like at the market. They're not mistrustful, they pour out their merchandise any which way. They don't know how to present things properly. You don't really have time to search through their things, you pass on, you don't go back, you're in a hurry yourself. That must make them sad. Maybe they pack up again? Or just abandon their things? I don't know. What becomes of them? We don't have a clue. Maybe they set off again until nothing's left? And then where do they go? Life is enormous all the same. You can lose yourself anywhere.

Index of recurrent characters

AGATHE: see L'ESPINASSE (MADEMOISELLE).

ANGÈLE: prostitute, wife of Cascade (Bébert); Cascade says she is eighteen, but she later says that she's two years older than Ferdinand, who must be twenty. Her character, also present in *Londres*, prefigures Angèle, the wife of Cascade Farcy, in *Guignol's Band*.

BÉBERT (GONTRAN): he becomes Gontran Cascade and says his name is actually Julien Boisson. He ends up executed. In *Guignol's Band*, a nephew of Cascade Farcy, Raoul (who becomes Roger, Cascade's brother), is executed for his self-inflicted wounds.

CASCADE: see BÉBERT.

DES ENTRAYES, GENERAL, here called MÉTULEU: Colonel (also General) Céladon des Entrayes in *Journey to the End of Night* and Des Entrayes in *Guignol's Band* and *Fable for Another Time*.

FERDINAND: narrator, Céline's alter ego.

GWENDOR: character in *La volonté du roi Krogold* (The Will of King Krogold), traitorous prince of Christiania, killed by King Krogold.

HARNACHE (MONSIEUR): insurance agent working in the same company as Ferdinand's father. His model is Paul Houzet de Boubers, agent for the insurance company Le Phénix, Céline's father's company, in Hazebrouck.

JOAD: character in *La volonté du roi Krogold*, lover of Wanda.

KERSUZON: cavalryman, comrade of Ferdinand, killed in battle. He also appears in *Journey to the End of Night* and in

Bagatelles pour un massacre [Trifles for a Massacre], and he is a main character in the recently discovered unpublished manuscript sections of *Cannon Fodder*.

KROGOLD: king of the legend of the same name, extracts of which appear in *Death on the Installment Plan*; this tale is among the rediscovered Céline manuscripts. Father of Wanda and killer of Gwendor, he owns a fortress called Morehande.

LE CAM: cavalryman, comrade of Ferdinand, killed in combat. He also appears in *Cannon Fodder*.

LE DRELLIÈRE: cavalryman, probably Ferdinand's adjutant, killed in combat.

L'ESPINASSE (MADEMOISELLE): nurse at Peurdu-sur-la-Lys. Called Aline, she could also be the Agathe mentioned at the end of the novel. Probably inspired by Alice David, the nurse in Hazebrouck with whom Céline is said to have had an affair.

MÉCONILLE: medical officer who operates on Ferdinand. The doctor who operated on Céline in Hazebrouck was named Gabriel Sénellart. Even though the name sometimes looks like Mécouille in the manuscript, Méconille is the most likely spelling.

MOTHER OF FERDINAND: called by her husband, Ferdinand's father, Célestine, then Clémence (as in *Death on the Installment Plan*).

MORVAN: character in *La volonté du roi Krogold*; father of Joad, he is killed by Thibaut.

ONIME (MADAME): canteen worker. In *Cannon Fodder*, Madame Leurbanne, the woman who works in the canteen, is suspected of having an affair with the adjutant Lacadent.

FATHER OF FERDINAND: like Monsieur Harnache, he works at La Coccinelle, the equivalent of Le Phénix, the insurance company in which Fernand Destouches worked.

PURCELL: Major Cecil B. Purcell K. B. B., engineer; a client of Angèle, it's thanks to him that Ferdinand and Angèle can go to London. He also appears as one of the characters in *Londres* (London).

THIBAUT: troubadour, character in *La volonté du roi Krogold*; he kills Morvan, the father of Joad.

WANDA (PRINCESS): daughter of King Krogold, a character in *La volonté du roi Krogold*.

New Directions Paperbooks—a partial listing

Kaouther Adimi, Our Riches
Adonis, Songs of Mihyar the Damascene
César Aira, Ghosts
  An Episode in the Life of a Landscape Painter
Will Alexander, Refractive Africa
Osama Alomar, The Teeth of the Comb
Guillaume Apollinaire, Selected Writings
Jessica Au, Cold Enough for Snow
Paul Auster, The Red Notebook
Ingeborg Bachmann, Malina
Honoré de Balzac, Colonel Chabert
Djuna Barnes, Nightwood
Charles Baudelaire, The Flowers of Evil*
Bei Dao, City Gate, Open Up
Mei-Mei Berssenbrugge, Empathy
Max Blecher, Adventures in Immediate Irreality
Roberto Bolaño, By Night in Chile
  Distant Star
Jorge Luis Borges, Labyrinths
  Seven Nights
Beatriz Bracher, Antonio
Coral Bracho, Firefly Under the Tongue*
Kamau Brathwaite, Ancestors
Basil Bunting, Complete Poems
Anne Carson, Glass, Irony & God
  Norma Jeane Baker of Troy
Horacio Castellanos Moya, Senselessness
Camilo José Cela, Mazurka for Two Dead Men
Louis-Ferdinand Céline
  Death on the Installment Plan
  Journey to the End of the Night
Rafael Chirbes, Cremation
Inger Christensen, alphabet
Julio Cortázar, Cronopios & Famas
Jonathan Creasy (ed.), Black Mountain Poems
Robert Creeley, If I Were Writing This
Guy Davenport, 7 Greeks
Amparo Davila, The Houseguest
Osamu Dazai, No Longer Human
  The Setting Sun
H.D., Selected Poems
Helen DeWitt, The Last Samurai
  Some Trick
Marcia Douglas
  The Marvellous Equations of the Dread
Daša Drndić, EEG
Robert Duncan, Selected Poems

Eça de Queirós, The Maias
William Empson, 7 Types of Ambiguity
Mathias Énard, Compass
Shusaku Endo, Deep River
Jenny Erpenbeck, The End of Days
  Go, Went, Gone
Lawrence Ferlinghetti
  A Coney Island of the Mind
Thalia Field, Personhood
F. Scott Fitzgerald, The Crack-Up
  On Booze
Emilio Fraia, Sevastopol
Jean Frémon, Now, Now, Louison
Rivka Galchen, Little Labors
Forrest Gander, Be With
Romain Gary, The Kites
Natalia Ginzburg, The Dry Heart
  Happiness, as Such
Henry Green, Concluding
Felisberto Hernández, Piano Stories
Hermann Hesse, Siddhartha
Takashi Hiraide, The Guest Cat
Yoel Hoffmann, Moods
Susan Howe, My Emily Dickinson
  Concordance
Bohumil Hrabal, I Served the King of England
Qurratulain Hyder, River of Fire
Sonallah Ibrahim, That Smell
Rachel Ingalls, Mrs. Caliban
Christopher Isherwood, The Berlin Stories
Fleur Jaeggy, Sweet Days of Discipline
Alfred Jarry, Ubu Roi
B.S. Johnson, House Mother Normal
James Joyce, Stephen Hero
Franz Kafka, Amerika: The Man Who Disappeared
Yasunari Kawabata, Dandelions
John Keene, Counternarratives
Heinrich von Kleist, Michael Kohlhaas
Alexander Kluge, Temple of the Scapegoat
Wolfgang Koeppen, Pigeons on the Grass
Taeko Kono, Toddler-Hunting
Laszlo Krasznahorkai, Satantango
  Seiobo There Below
Ryszard Krynicki, Magnetic Point
Eka Kurniawan, Beauty Is a Wound
Mme. de Lafayette, The Princess of Clèves
Lautréamont, Maldoror

Siegfried Lenz, The German Lesson
Alexander Lernet-Holenia, Count Luna
Denise Levertov, Selected Poems
Li Po, Selected Poems
Clarice Lispector, The Hour of the Star
  The Passion According to G. H.
Federico García Lorca, Selected Poems*
Nathaniel Mackey, Splay Anthem
Xavier de Maistre, Voyage Around My Room
Stéphane Mallarmé, Selected Poetry and Prose*
Javier Marías, Your Face Tomorrow (3 volumes)
Adam Mars-Jones, Box Hill
Bernadette Mayer, Midwinter Day
Carson McCullers, The Member of the Wedding
Fernando Melchor, Hurricane Season
Thomas Merton, New Seeds of Contemplation
  The Way of Chuang Tzu
Henri Michaux, A Barbarian in Asia
Dunya Mikhail, The Beekeeper
Henry Miller, The Colossus of Maroussi
  Big Sur & the Oranges of Hieronymus Bosch
Yukio Mishima, Confessions of a Mask
  Death in Midsummer
Eugenio Montale, Selected Poems*
Vladimir Nabokov, Laughter in the Dark
  Nikolai Gogol
Pablo Neruda, The Captain's Verses*
  Love Poems*
Charles Olson, Selected Writings
George Oppen, New Collected Poems
Wilfred Owen, Collected Poems
Hiroko Oyamada, The Hole
José Emilio Pacheco, Battles in the Desert
Michael Palmer, Little Elegies for Sister Satan
Nicanor Parra, Antipoems*
Boris Pasternak, Safe Conduct
Octavio Paz, Poems of Octavio Paz
Victor Pelevin, Omon Ra
Georges Perec, Ellis Island
Alejandra Pizarnik
  Extracting the Stone of Madness
Ezra Pound, The Cantos
  New Selected Poems and Translations
Raymond Queneau, Exercises in Style
Qian Zhongshu, Fortress Besieged
Herbert Read, The Green Child
Kenneth Rexroth, Selected Poems
Keith Ridgway, A Shock

Rainer Maria Rilke
  Poems from the Book of Hours
Arthur Rimbaud, Illuminations*
  A Season in Hell and The Drunken Boat*
Evelio Rosero, The Armies
Fran Ross, Oreo
Joseph Roth, The Emperor's Tomb
Raymond Roussel, Locus Solus
Ihara Saikaku, The Life of an Amorous Woman
Nathalie Sarraute, Tropisms
Jean-Paul Sartre, Nausea
Judith Schalansky, An Inventory of Losses
Delmore Schwartz
  In Dreams Begin Responsibilities
W. G. Sebald, The Emigrants
  The Rings of Saturn
Anne Serre, The Governesses
Patti Smith, Woolgathering
Stevie Smith, Best Poems
  Novel on Yellow Paper
Gary Snyder, Turtle Island
Dag Solstad, Professor Andersen's Night
Muriel Spark, The Driver's Seat
Maria Stepanova, In Memory of Memory
Wislawa Szymborska, How to Start Writing
Antonio Tabucchi, Pereira Maintains
Junichiro Tanizaki, The Maids
Yoko Tawada, The Emissary
  Memoirs of a Polar Bear
Dylan Thomas, A Child's Christmas in Wales
  Collected Poems
Tomas Tranströmer, The Great Enigma
Leonid Tsypkin, Summer in Baden-Baden
Tu Fu, Selected Poems
Paul Valéry, Selected Writings
Enrique Vila-Matas, Bartleby & Co.
Elio Vittorini, Conversations in Sicily
Rosmarie Waldrop, The Nick of Time
Robert Walser, The Assistant
  The Tanners
Eliot Weinberger, An Elemental Thing
  The Ghosts of Birds
Nathanael West, The Day of the Locust
  Miss Lonelyhearts
Tennessee Williams, The Glass Menagerie
  A Streetcar Named Desire
William Carlos Williams, Selected Poems
Louis Zukofsky, "A"

*BILINGUAL EDITION

For a complete listing, request a free catalog from New Directions, 80 8th Avenue, New York, NY 10011
or visit us online at **ndbooks.com**